ADVENTURE
at
SIMBA HILL

ADVENTURE
at
SIMBA HILL

$\mathcal{S}$USAN $\mathcal{R}$UNHOLT

VIKING
An Imprint of Penguin Group (USA) Inc.

VIKING

Published by Penguin Group

Penguin Group (USA) Inc., 345 Hudson Street, New York, New York 10014, U.S.A.

Penguin Group (Canada), 90 Eglinton Avenue East, Suite 700, Toronto, Ontario, Canada

M4P 2Y3 (a division of Pearson Penguin Canada Inc.)

Penguin Books Ltd, 80 Strand, London WC2R 0RL, England

Penguin Ireland, 25 St Stephen's Green, Dublin 2, Ireland (a division of Penguin Books Ltd)

Penguin Group (Australia), 250 Camberwell Road, Camberwell, Victoria 3124, Australia

(a division of Pearson Australia Group Pty Ltd)

Penguin Books India Pvt Ltd, 11 Community Centre, Panchsheel Park, New Delhi – 110 017, India

Penguin Group (NZ), 67 Apollo Drive, Rosedale, North Shore 0745, New Zealand

(a division of Pearson New Zealand Ltd.)

Penguin Books (South Africa) (Pty) Ltd, 24 Sturdee Avenue, Rosebank, Johannesburg 2196, South Africa

Penguin Books Ltd, Registered Offices: 80 Strand, London WC2R 0RL, England

First published in 2011 by Viking, a member of Penguin Group (USA) Inc.

10 9 8 7 6 5 4 3 2 1

LIBRARY OF CONGRESS CATALOGING-IN-PUBLICATION DATA IS AVAILABLE

ISBN: 978-0-670-01201-5

Printed in USA   Set in CG Cloister

To Tom and Muriel, Patty,
Benson, Bernard,
and the others with whom I shared Africa

ADVENTURE
at
SIMBA HILL

1

Camellia, Lucas, and the Personal Cooling System

ONE WORD and i hack u 2 pieces and throw u 2 the hyenas.

One word about what?

I stared at my phone. The text was from my best friend, Lucas Stickney. We're both girls.

I texted back, *wtm?* That stood for *what the meep? Meep* is what Lucas and I substitute for the kind of words fourteen-year-olds like us aren't allowed to say in front of adults, and using it has kind of gotten to be a habit.

The text came back. *STARVING hyenas.*

I still had no clue.

It was a snowy Sunday afternoon in December. Mom was on the other end of the couch leafing through a magazine as we watched old *30 Rock* episodes from Netflix. She must have seen my expression out of the corner of her eye, because she looked up from the page and said, "What's going on?"

I did a palms up, but before I could tell her, I heard people coming up the stairs to our duplex. The next second there was a knock.

The minute I opened the door I understood.

Lucas was on the landing. Starting at the bottom and working my way to the top, she was wearing: a pair of hiking boots, the kind made for summer, with vents on the sides (her feet must have been freezing in the cold Minnesota weather); a pair of something like cargo pants stuffed into the boots, with bunches of pockets, and zippers around the calves and around the thighs so you could turn them into cropped pants or Bermuda shorts; a white shirt with sleeves that could be rolled up and buttoned with a tab to make them short sleeves; and a journalist vest, with even more pockets than the pants. And to top it all off, one of those safari helmet things. It was hard and white, with a strap under the chin and—I couldn't believe it—a little bitty fan on an arm hanging over the brim right in front.

Lucas stood there for approximately twenty seconds, staring at me, her eyes daring me to say a single word.

I tried not to smile as I took it all in, but I'm not sure I managed it. Mom was standing behind me. I wondered if *she* was able to keep a straight face.

Finally Camellia's head popped out from behind Lucas. "I wanted to give y'all time to get the full effect," she said in that big Southern accent she uses when she remembers.

Camellia—or, as Lucas calls her, the Fair Camellia—is Lucas's mom.

"Doesn't she look like she's just come out of the African shrub?"

Lucas rolled her eyes. "It's bush, Mom. African bush."

"Bush, shrub, whatever."

"Come in! It's cold in the stairwell!" Mom said. From the sound of her voice, I was almost one hundred percent positive she was trying not to laugh.

I should explain about Camellia. First off, she's beautiful. She has red hair and long legs and big blue eyes, and she spends at least two hours every day working out with her own personal trainer, so she's gorgeous. As for her accent, she's lived in Saint Paul for more than seventeen years, so sometimes she forgets to use it and it goes away almost completely.

Camellia loves Lucas and her brother, who Lucas calls the Brat Child, but she seems to love shopping almost as much as she loves her kids. She's totally into looks and clothes. The problem is, Lucas is totally *not* into looks *or* clothes.

When Lucas and her mom were in the living room and the door was closed behind them, my mom managed to come up with, "That's a very impressive outfit you're wearing, Lucas."

Lucas kept drilling me with the look that I knew meant something about feeding pieces of me to starving hyenas, so I kept my mouth shut and tried to look enthused.

Camellia was holding Lucas's winter coat draped over a stack of gift-wrapped packages. Mom took the pile and put it on the coffee table.

"I had just the friendliest clerk at REI," Camellia gushed as she waved away Mom's offer to take her full-length fur. "He was cute, too. He just showed me every little thing Lucas would need for goin' on safari. All the fabrics are made to stay cool in hot weather, and they can be washed out in the sink and dry in *no* time."

"And the pith helmet? Did that come from REI?" Mom asked.

Pith helmet? Was that what it was really called?

Camellia turned to gaze at the hat with something like rapture. Lucas was looking up cross-eyed at the fan.

"No, I found that in a special catalog," Camellia said. "It's a personal cooling system! Don't you just *love* it? I thought it was so *practical*. I mean, in Kenya, the girls are going to be at the equator. It's *hot* at the equator."

No meep, Sherlock.

Camellia looked at Lucas and clasped her gloved hands together. "Okay, honey, show 'em!"

Lucas rolled her eyes again. "MO-om!"

"C'mon, punkin, it's the best part!"

Lucas looked at me again. Her expression had changed. Now it said, "Please save me!" Then she reached up under the hat brim and flipped a little switch, and the fan started blowing on her face.

I smiled. I couldn't help it.

Lucas said with mock enthusiasm, "There's an outfit just like this for you, too. Including the hat."

The thought knocked the smile off my face.

Camellia took the wrapped packages from the coffee table, handed a small one to Mom, and gave the rest of the stack to me. "I figured that since Allen and I were responsible for gettin' your uncle to take you along on his trip, the least we could do would be to provide one of your outfits. Merry Christmas, from our family to yours."

Mom, obviously trying hard to keep from laughing, said, "What do you say, hon?"

I realized I was standing there with my mouth open. "Um, thank you so much for the . . . really thoughtful gift, Camellia."

"Well, we'd better run. I have more gifts to deliver. Lucas, are you comin'?"

"Why don't you stay?" I asked. "We're watching *30 Rock*."

"Yeah, you can hang out," Mom said. "We're going to have pizza later. Cossetta's."

"Yum. If it's Cossetta's I'm staying. If that's okay." She looked at her mom.

"I'll just get along, then," Camellia said.

"We'll see you again before the holiday." Mom opened the door for her.

"Merry Christmas to y'all," Camellia said. "Bah-*baah*." (That's *bye-bye* in Camellia language.) She disappeared, her mink dragging on the stairs behind her. I wondered how anybody could walk on Minnesota's ice in boots with five-inch heels, but if anybody could do it, it would be Camellia.

Mom closed the door. Lucas leaned against it, pulled off the hat, sighed, and closed her eyes like a drama queen. "Welcome to my world."

I should probably explain why Camellia was shopping for Lucas at REI, instead of Nordstrom's, like usual. My uncle Geoff was going to Kenya over Christmas vacation. He was going to a cave where some archaeologists had been digging up artifacts. (That's what they call the art and pots and other things they find in really ancient sites.) He's an archaeology professor at the University of Minnesota, and he's always running off to where somebody is digging up treasures from thousands of years ago. He was making this trip to join one of his former students, who'd been working most of the year at this archaeological dig at a place called Simba Hill.

Lucas had been thinking and talking about Africa every chance she got since the monthlong Africa Awareness Project at the school she goes to. So of course when she found out Uncle Geoff was going to Kenya, she told Camellia, and her dad, Allen the Meep. Lucas's dad is a famous attorney who goes all over the world working for clients. He almost always wins his cases because he's one of the world's greatest arguers. If arguers is even a word.

Well, first thing you know, Allen sets up this private meeting with Uncle Geoff where he asks if Lucas and I can go along on the trip. The deal was that Lucas's super-rich family would pay for both of us, because, first, they want Lucas to have all of these experiences, which they think will help her get into Harvard, and second, it would be their way of thanking me for being such a good friend to Lucas and even saving her life once.

As an added bonus, Allen said he would make a large donation to help pay for the archaeological dig itself. Archaeologists are always looking for money to fund their work.

Well, that did it. Uncle Geoff immediately said yes.

(I know that Allen doesn't sound much like a meep when I say all this, but he really is one. Take my word for it.)

Anyway, a couple of days after Christmas, there Lucas and I were with Uncle Geoff, in Africa, on safari, with dangerous wild animals running around loose, in the middle of a ring of smugglers that was almost more dangerous than the animals, and—well, that's what this story is about.

2

The Dark Continent

"Did you know that pretty much everyone in Kenya is trilingual?" Lucas asked. "At home they speak whatever their native language is, at school they speak English, and they use Swahili, or what they would call Kiswahili, to communicate with people of other tribes. And the safari guides speak even more languages. Some of them speak as many as six or seven."

We were in the airplane on our way to Kenya. We'd been flying for most of two days, and Lucas had been telling me facts like this about Africa almost the whole way. Every time I woke up from a nap or lifted my head from the homework I was doing for the days of school I was going to miss, it was just fact after fact after fact.

"Did you know that the Sahara Desert is nearly as big as the whole United States, including Alaska and Hawaii?" And, "Did you know that the Masai Mara is the most popular game reserve in Kenya?" And, "Did you know that there are more than four hundred fifty species just of birds . . ."

I didn't care how many species of birds there were. I stopped listening and looked out the window.

The sun had gone down at least an hour before, and since then we'd flown over hundreds, maybe thousands of miles where there were absolutely no city lights below us. No lights from small towns, no lights from farms. The earth was all completely black, lit by only fires. One fire here, one there, as far as you could see. I wondered who the people were who sat around those fires. That was the kind of thing that was interesting to me.

Lucas is unbelievably smart. She has a lightning-swift brain and a photographic memory, which means she can remember everything she's ever seen. Maybe it's because of all that big, huge mental power, I don't know, but she can get really focused on one thing. Last summer, she'd been obsessed with a guy named Josh Daniels that she'd had a crush on. Now it was all Africa, all the time. I *almost* missed Josh.

Like I said, it started with that Africa Awareness Project at the private academy she goes to. (I go to a public school.) For the entire month of October, almost every one of her classes had something to do with Africa—reading, science, social studies, art—and they had special dance programs, and concerts with music from different countries, and library programs with authors who wrote about Africa . . . well, that gives you an idea.

Plus, every kid in her school had to raise money to help the people of Africa. The rule was they had to do it without getting any money from their relatives. Lucas and her project partner decided to give their money to Heifer International, which buys livestock for poor families. They washed cars, babysat, and did yard work, and between the two of them they came up with enough to buy a cow for a family in Tanzania. I thought that part was pretty cool, and I even helped her with some of the yard work.

During this time, Lucas had become a total Africa fanatic. She had two billion facts about the whole continent stored in her brain, and she was constantly giving me these mini-lectures about African history and government and tribes and natural resources and animals. Which could be something interesting, or could be, like, whether the nation of Kenya produced large quantities of manganese.

When I mentioned to Mom how much the mini-lectures were getting on my nerves, she said, "I get why that would drive you nuts. But it's not going to do you any good to complain to *me* about it. Why don't you say something about it to Lucas?"

I knew I should, but I kept putting it off, hoping—I don't know what. Maybe hoping Lucas would run out of things to tell me.

Of course, she didn't. In fact, the closer we got to our trip, the more mini-lectures she delivered. And then it was time for us to leave, and I still hadn't said anything.

Finally, as we waited at the airport to catch the flight that would take us from our home in Saint Paul to Nairobi, Kenya, I'd promised myself that when Lucas and I were alone, I'd talk to her about the mini-lectures. Now Lucas, Uncle Geoff, and I were sitting together on the airplane (we'd taken turns sitting at the window), and Uncle Geoff was sound asleep. It was time.

I turned to her, told myself to have courage and stop being such a wimp, and started in.

"Lucas, look at this," I said, and pulled back so she could lean over me and look out the window.

She'd been talking about Africa for weeks, but now that she saw the real thing, she was quiet. Finally she said, "No wonder they call it the Dark Continent."

She unbuckled her seatbelt and half stood. She had a better view that way, and I could look down, too. We stayed like that, totally quiet, for a long time.

While she was still standing there, I took a breath and launched in. "Lucas, I've learned a ton about Africa from you." I wanted to add, *and at least some of it was really interesting*. But I didn't.

"But now that we're here, what I want to do is just . . . just *be* here and soak it up. I want to see and experience it. I don't want to know every single thing about it. I mean . . . now that we're here," I repeated, sounding totally lame.

"Are you asking me not to tell you so much about Africa?" Trust Lucas to cut to the chase.

"It's not that I don't want you to tell me *anything* more about Africa. You know a lot of really interesting things. It's just that mostly I want to look and listen and just, like, *be* here. I already know a ton about Kenya, and a lot of that I've learned from you. And I'm really grateful, but—"

Lucas plunked back down in her seat. "But what you're saying is that what's down there," she said, pointing to the ground, "is a whole lot more interesting than how many languages our safari guide might speak. Okay, I can kind of get that. I'll try to keep my mouth shut about facts. But you'll have to give me a break if a couple of times I just can't help myself."

"Deal," I said.

Whew, she wasn't mad at me. What a relief! But when I thought about it, I shouldn't have been surprised. When Lucas knows somebody else is right, she admits it right away. It's one of about a million reasons why she's my best friend and I love her.

3

"It's a Mystery"

"You know, much as I like your mom, it's going to be fun being here without her," Lucas said.

"Yeah, here we are, actually in Nairobi, Kenya, in Africa, and we're kind of on our own. It feels . . . it feels like—"

"An adventure!" Lucas finished for me.

"That's it exactly! An adventure!" I added, knocking at Uncle Geoff's door.

We were in our hotel in Nairobi, and Lucas, Uncle Geoff, and I were going to go to breakfast together.

"I wonder if the people in the dining room will be dressed in the same kind of clothes as the people in the airport," she said.

I thought about the bright colors of the outfits a lot of the people had been wearing when we landed the night before, and how different they were from the woolly sweaters and huge, puffy coats people wore in Minnesota in December.

When we got down to the hotel dining room, it turned out to be just as colorful as I'd hoped it would be. Yeah, there were a lot of guys sitting around in suits, but the place was also full of men and women wearing the tribal dress we'd seen at the airport and on the streets. The tablecloths all had what must have been traditional African patterns—some green, some blue, some yellow—and there were huge color pictures of animals on the walls.

Charlie, Uncle Geoff's former student who'd met our plane the night before, was sitting alone at a table in the corner.

He stood up when he saw Uncle Geoff, Lucas, and me walk in. "*Jambo*. You all look so rested and refreshed compared to when I left you last night. How did you all sleep?"

We said we'd slept well. In fact, after all the flying, I didn't even remember my head hitting the pillow.

Charlie was American, white, and very, very tall. Probably five inches taller than Uncle Geoff, who's just under six feet. He was extremely skinny, wore round glasses, and instead of smiling when he or somebody else made a joke, he'd raise his eyebrows, or his mustache would twitch.

"Are we expecting others?" Uncle Geoff asked, looking at the two empty places.

"Just one. Professor Wanjohi is going to join us. He's

been with some family members here in Nairobi for the holiday, and he'll meet us for breakfast."

"Wonderful!" Uncle Geoff said, and turned to Lucas and me. "That's the archaeologist I told you about. The one who's leading the dig. I met him last year at the conference in Vienna. A very important man in his particular field. President of the African Rock Art Association."

Charlie nodded. "He also heads the Rock Art Institute at the University of Witwatersrand, in Johannesburg, South Africa, which is really the leading university in the field. But he's originally from Kenya. Plus, he's a pretty nice guy. Even if he does assign me all the drudge work." Charlie raised his eyebrows, looked over his glasses, then down at his menu.

The waiter came and was pouring coffee for the guys when Uncle Geoff caught sight of someone coming toward us.

He smiled and stood up. "Professor Wanjohi, good to see you again!"

The professor was on the short side, and a little stocky. He had dark, dark skin like all the black people we'd seen in Kenya so far, white hair cut close to his scalp, and bright brown eyes behind wire-rimmed glasses. He took hold of Uncle Geoff's arm with one hand as he pumped his hand with the other. It was obvious just from this much that the professor was full of energy—standing there next to him, I could almost feel it radiating off him—and that he loved being around people.

"The pleasure is mine, Geoff. But last time we met, you agreed to call me David." He spoke with a British accent.

Uncle Geoff turned to us. "Girls, this is Professor David Wanjohi. David, this is my niece, Kari Sundgren, and her friend Lucas Stickney."

"Hello Kari, hello Lucas," the professor said as he shook our hands.

"Nice to meet you," I said with a blush.

Lucas said the same thing, only of course she didn't blush. She doesn't have one single shy cell in her body.

The professor looked from Uncle Geoff to me. "There's quite a family resemblance."

"People do seem to think so," Uncle Geoff said. The three of us—Mom, Uncle Geoff, and I—all have black, curly hair, and green or hazel eyes. Nobody would ever think that Lucas, who has curly reddish blonde hair and blue eyes, could be my sister.

The professor took a chair, we gave the waiter our drink orders—I ordered passion fruit juice just because of the name—and everyone studied the menu. There were lots of familiar things, but also a section called KENYAN SPECIALTIES.

"What's *mandazi*?" I asked.

"To you they would be like squarish, flattish dough-nuts," the professor answered. "They're what most people eat for breakfast in Kenya."

"Sweet potatoes? For breakfast?" Lucas was looking at another thing listed in the Kenyan section.

"The professor and I have a running disagreement about the sweet potatoes," Charlie said, looking at Lucas and me solemnly over his glasses. "These are served plain, with nothing on them. I say sweet potatoes need butter and salt to be edible, and are improved by a touch of brown sugar and pecans." He raised his eyebrows a couple of times in our direction.

"The very idea is outrageous!" Professor Wanjohi responded, and both men looked at us with twinkling eyes, obviously enjoying their argument.

The waiter came with our drinks and a tray of fruit chunks. The fruit was bright, with watermelon, kiwi, orange sections, pineapple, strawberries, and mango, and just added to the colorfulness of the room. We all gave our orders. I decided against the sweet potatoes—I like them with butter, too—but I did order a *mandazi*, along with some scrambled eggs and sausages.

"Are you looking forward to your time in Africa?" the professor asked as we handed over our menus.

Lucas answered first, because I'd just popped a strawberry in my mouth.

"Even what we've seen already totally rocks!" She told him about the campfires visible from the airplane the night before.

"In tribal villages, they make sure the fires stay lighted

all night to keep the wild animals away," the professor said.

"Wow! That makes everything we have in Minnesota seem so kind of . . . tame," I said.

Professor Wanjohi grinned. "That's what makes international travel so fascinating, isn't it? Seeing the new things. Is this the first place you two have been outside the United States?"

We both shook our heads, and between the two of us, we told him about visiting London, Paris, Amsterdam, and different parts of Scotland.

"But those places are all in Western Europe," he said, "and the United States and Canada take their way of life from Europe. Africa is completely different.

"I felt the difference in reverse when I was a young man and went to Oxford to go to university. Everything about England was completely different from Africa. The buildings, the clothing, the customs, the food. There were church bells! I'd never heard church bells. The weather was *awful*." The professor closed his eyes tight and shook his head as if the memory was almost too much for him. "It seemed to be cold and rainy all the time. But I was fascinated. Later I started going to Asia, and that's just as different from Africa as Europe or America is, only in a whole new way."

Just then the waiter came with our meals.

"What are you eager to see while you're here?" Charlie asked.

Again, Lucas was first to answer. "We can't wait to see the animals. But I really want to see members of the different tribes. I'm especially interested in the Maasai culture. I hope to visit a Maasai village while I'm here."

"How about you, Kari?" Charlie asked. "What are you looking forward to?"

"Well, I'm hoping I get a chance to see the site where you guys are working."

"Kari wants to become an archaeologist," Uncle Geoff said.

"An archaeologist! Really!" Charlie held up his coffee cup so the waiter could give him a refill. "It all becomes clear to me now. Your uncle has been brainwashing you since birth."

"Absolutely!" Uncle Geoff said. "That's why girls have uncles."

"You'll have to come out and pay us some long visits," the professor said. "Have you ever visited a dig?"

I shook my head. "Not yet. Uncle Geoff has taught me a lot about archaeology, though. How artifacts help us understand the way people lived thousands of years ago."

"I tell her that when they dig up artifacts from her generation, all they're going to find are computers and cell phones and iPods," Uncle Geoff said.

The professor was still smiling at Uncle Geoff's remark when his cell phone rang. He got up and left the table.

Because of where I was sitting I could see him go over

to a quiet corner near the entrance to the restaurant. I wasn't really paying attention to him. I was busy eating. The *mandazi* wasn't quite as sweet as a doughnut, but it wasn't bad. As I chowed down on my sausage and eggs, I listened to Charlie and Uncle Geoff talk about what was still left to do at the Simba Hill dig in the next couple weeks before the team finished.

When I happened to glance up in the professor's direction again, I was surprised by the expression on his face. He was listening and frowning as if something was really, really wrong.

He had stepped over to a wooden rack where there were newspapers for people in the restaurant to read. With his free hand he pulled one of the papers off, set it down on an empty table, and opened it to the second page. After a few more minutes he snapped the phone shut and came back to the table with the newspaper.

Uncle Geoff broke off in the middle of his sentence when he saw the professor's expression. "Something wrong?" he asked.

"Terribly." Still on his feet, Professor Wanjohi moved his dishes aside to make room for the paper. Charlie, who had the chair next to him, shoved his own dishes, too.

"That was one of my colleagues from the Rock Art Association," Professor Wanjohi said. "Last night, London customs officials arrested a man who'd flown in from Nairobi with a suitcase full of stolen rock art. There's a story in the paper, and a photograph. Look." He spread the newspaper out in the cleared space and pointed to a photo. It showed a rock with a picture scratched into it. It was a very simple drawing, but beautiful, and you could tell the animal was a rhinoceros.

He thumped the newspaper photo with his finger. "This is exactly like the art we've been finding." He lifted his head. "We'll have to conduct scientific tests, of course, but at first blush it looks very much like someone is looting artifacts from the Simba Hill site."

Charlie sat back in his chair, a stunned expression on his face. "Do they have any idea how it was done or who was in on it?"

The professor shook his head. "It's a mystery."

Lucas looked at me, her eyes wide. Nothing got our attention more than those three little words.

4

We Don't Have That in Minnesota

Professor Wanjohi folded up the paper, rearranged his plate and silverware, and sat back down. "Charlie, you and I had better get back right away and find out if anything is missing." He turned to the rest of us. "We're traveling by plane. It's a four-seater, so Geoff, if you want to ride along . . ."

For a second I wondered why there wouldn't be two places empty, but then I remembered the pilot.

"Go ahead, Uncle Geoff. We want to see the countryside. Right, Lucas?"

"Totally!" Lucas said.

Uncle Geoff shook his head. "No way I'm abandoning you on our first morning in Africa. My sister would crucify me."

"We'll be okay!" Lucas said. "We *are* fourteen years old."

"Uncle Geoff, I know you. After what you just heard, you're dying to get out to the dig site!"

He opened his mouth, but before he could protest, Charlie said, "I don't want to interfere here, but Bernard is a superb safari driver, and a terrific guy to boot."

Bernard was our driver and safari guide. He'd driven us from the airport in his van the night before.

The professor nodded. "I've hired him as a driver every time I've been in Kenya for at least the past ten years. I can vouch for him absolutely."

Uncle Geoff looked at Lucas and me. "Are you sure you wouldn't mind?"

"C'mon, Geoff," Charlie said. "When have kids their age ever wanted more than the absolute minimum of adults around?"

It was all I could do not to smile, because that's exactly what I'd been thinking.

"Go! I know you want to!" I said. "When I e-mail Mom I promise to forget to mention that you're not riding out with us."

"Sounds like an excellent plan," Charlie said.

Uncle Geoff shrugged. "I guess I'm outnumbered." And with a grin that looked both guilty and excited, he took off to get repacked.

Fifteen minutes later he reappeared downstairs, dragging his suitcase across the lobby to where Lucas and I stood with Charlie and Bernard, the driver. Bernard had a white smile so bright it almost glowed, hair cut close to his scalp, and dark eyes that were big and kind and friendly. According to what Charlie had said, he'd done a lot of driving for the Simba Hill team and been a part-time guard, but for the weeks Lucas and I were in Kenya, he'd be mostly assigned to us.

The professor had been standing in the corner making calls on his cell phone. When he saw Uncle Geoff get out of the elevator, he snapped the phone shut and joined us.

"Very good news," he said, although the news wasn't good enough to make him smile. "I got a call from Maria, the other archaeologist who's been working with us. She said everyone at the lodge was talking about the newspaper story when she went down for breakfast, so she immediately went out to the dig site to take a look. She says none of the artifacts we've unearthed so far is missing, and the dig site itself has not been disturbed."

"Any information about the suspect or the crime itself?" Charlie asked.

The professor shook his head. "I spoke with a police representative. They've only begun their investigation. The man they caught in London was from Nairobi, but at this point they know very little beyond that."

Uncle Geoff excused himself to go pay our hotel bill, and Bernard went outside to pull the van up to the entrance.

"If none of the rocks you've dug up was taken, where are these rocks coming from?" Lucas asked the professor.

"Assuming the rocks *are* from Simba Hill, there must be another entrance to the cave where additional specimens can be found. We haven't been able to explore where the cave passages might lead because they've collapsed over the centuries."

"Um, this might be a really stupid question, but why is this such a big deal?" Lucas asked. "I mean, if whatever the guy smuggled into London wouldn't have been found by anybody else, why is it so bad that somebody dug it up and took it out of the country?"

"That's not a stupid question, Lucas. The fact is, these pieces are the relics of a civilization that existed thousands of years ago. Every piece can be a clue to the way human beings lived at that site, at that time. And you must remember, just because we have not yet discovered an archaeological site doesn't mean that future generations won't find it. To plunder even an unknown site is like destroying a piece of human history. The people who take pieces like this care nothing about the history or culture of the area, they just want to sell what they steal for as much money as they can get. Money. Profit. That's all that matters to them," he said, and you could tell from his voice how much he hated the thought of these people and their greed.

With the hotel bill paid, Uncle Geoff rejoined us. "Okay, girls," he said. "Are you all set? You have your money and passports, right?"

"In our money belts," I said.

He turned to the others. "How long is the trip by car?"

"About five hours to the lodge," Charlie said. "Another forty-five minutes beyond that to the dig site."

"Bernard, you'll call and let us know when you've made it to the lodge?" Uncle Geoff asked.

"Of course!" Bernard responded.

"Okay, kiddos, you're on your own for the day. I'll see you tonight."

The professor, trying for some of his former perkiness, said, "Be sure and keep track of everything that's not like Minnesota. I want a complete report."

Lucas and I looked at each other. We were on our way!

To be honest, after what had been in the newspaper, part of me was anxious to get out to where the artifacts had been stolen. Even though we might never solve the mystery, I was still intrigued by those three little words, after all.

But I was just as anxious to see what Kenya was all about. I'd spent weeks and weeks dreaming about what it would be like and what we'd see here. I had to admit, much as I'd hated Lucas's mini-lectures, a lot of what she'd told me was actually interesting and made me even more eager to visit than I would have been otherwise.

Anyway, by the time we'd been on the streets of Nairobi for five minutes, I was so busy looking at everything there was to see around me that I forgot all about the missing rocks.

Nairobi had normal buildings—no fancy architecture or anything that looked really ancient—but there were a lot of hills and beautiful blooming trees. The streets were wide and jammed with more cars than could safely fit on the roads, causing complete chaos, and the sidewalks were full of pedestrians. Like the people who'd been in the breakfast room and on the sidewalk in front of the hotel, some wore traditional outfits, and some had clothes like you'd see in America.

The van was designed so that everyone in it could have a good view, with two seats on each side next to the windows, one behind the other, leaving an aisle down the middle, plus the seat across the back. Sort of like in buses back home, only a whole lot smaller.

We were stopped at a stoplight across the street from a Toyota dealer, when Lucas said, "Kari, come over and look."

I unfastened my seat belt, got up, and looked out her window. Right above the Toyota sign was a tree full of big white birds with huge bills.

"They're marabou storks," Bernard said.

There were probably twenty of them, just sitting there on the branches.

"We don't have *that* in Minnesota," I said, taking the professor's advice.

That started something we did through our whole
trip out to the Masai Mara that morning. Saying "we
don't have that in Minnesota" every time we saw something that was different from what we had at home got to
be like a game for Lucas and me. Especially when we saw
something that seriously rocked, we'd race each other to
say it.

We didn't say it when we saw men riding their bicycles
with bundles of sticks or wrapped up packages on their
bikes. But when we saw a man with a chair fastened to
the back of his bike, we turned to each other and said it
in unison.

Most of what we saw on that trip was totally cool, but
some parts made me sad. While we were still in Nairobi
we passed by a part of town where there were beautiful
houses behind big gates, but we also went through the
worst part of any town I'd ever seen anywhere. I once
went to an Indian reservation in South Dakota and the
people there were so poor it was terrible. This was way
worse. It was hard to look at.

I wouldn't have known what to say about this in front
of Bernard if it hadn't been for the Obama signs everywhere.

"Wow! You're still celebrating that Obama was elected," I said.

Bernard smiled. "Yes, we are proud that the son of a
Kenyan man was elected President of the United States.

I think more than anything it is something for people to feel hopeful about. Especially those in greatest poverty," he said, looking at the neighborhood around us.

"Didn't Kenya have a corrupt president who stole a lot of the country's money for himself?" Lucas asked.

"That is correct. President Moi. I am surprised you know this," Bernard said, looking at us in the van's giant rearview mirror.

I said, "Lucas knows a *lot* about Africa."

Lucas shrugged. "We studied it in school, and I was really interested."

"Very impressive." Bernard smiled into the mirror again.

Outside Nairobi there were hills and farms where we saw women harvesting tea from tea bushes. They were dressed in wraparound skirts made of print materials in almost every bright color you could think of, and blouses or T-shirts, and big headdresses like tall turbans.

It was at this point that I realized that we'd been in the car all that time without a single mini-lecture. So far, so good for Lucas.

The people in the countryside seemed to be as poor as the people in the bad parts of the city. We saw villages where the buildings were all shacks and people walked around barefoot. Farther away from Nairobi we saw families out gathering sticks by the side of the road.

We came around a curve, the van slowed to a stop,

and Bernard said, "Here is something else you do not have in Minnesota."

We were looking way, way, way down the side of the hill into a big, humongous valley, stretching as far as we could see.

"That must be the Great Rift Valley!" Lucas said, like she couldn't quite believe it. She quickly unfastened her seat belt and came over to my side of the van, which was the side closer to the view. "I wrote a report for school on the Great Rift Valley!" She was so excited she was almost shouting.

"We will make a very brief stop here and you can tell us about it," Bernard said, pulling over to drive into a viewing spot at the side of the road. "I am going to raise the top. Do not be afraid. The van does not bite." The next second there was a grinding noise and the roof moved slowly upward about two feet, like a flat lid being lifted off, and stayed there on little legs attached to spots around the rim.

"The roof is made this way so passengers can see the landscape and the animals without being separated from them by a window," Bernard said. "Inside the game park this is the only way you get a clear view, because except at the guest lodges you must not get out of the vehicle without an armed guide. It is too dangerous."

By this time we were standing up and looking out.

It was obvious to me that this was one of the times I

was going to have to let Lucas tell us everything she knew, because she was dying to do it.

Sure enough, when Bernard said, "Okay, Lucas, tell us about it," it was like she couldn't help herself.

She started in, talking really fast, which she does some-times when she's totally excited. "The Great Rift Valley is a four-thousand-mile-long crack in the crust of the earth. It starts up in Lebanon and Israel, in the Middle East, and runs all the way down the eastern side of Africa, through Ethiopia, Kenya, and Tanzania to Mozambique . . ."

She went on and on with a geography lesson, saying something about volcanoes, then starting in on tectonic plates.

Just because she had to tell us about it didn't mean I had to listen to every word. While she talked, I was busy looking at the enormous valley stretching all the way to the horizon. Instead of being green, like the mountains where we'd been, it was dry and brown and amazingly flat.

"In a few million years the whole continent will split in two," Lucas said, finishing the lecture.

"Tectonic plates, huh?" I muttered, pretending I'd been listening. "I see."

I wasn't sure I really did see. I'd learned in school that tectonic plates were big chunks in the earth's surface, and that they moved and made earthquakes, but I wasn't exactly sure how they would have made this valley. Still, I wasn't going to ask Lucas to explain anything more about them or about the history of the place or what Africa would be like millions of years from now because I figured she *would* explain. And by the time she got finished it would *be* a million years later and I could see for myself what the plates did.

Bernard turned the key in the van.

"Bernard, when do you think we'll start seeing the animals?" I asked. This was what *I* was interested in.

"It will not be long now," he said, as the van started up. "The Rift looks empty, but it is actually full of life."

The road led down, down, down, onto the flat plain of the valley floor. The temperature, which had been so comfortable at a higher altitude, was suddenly uncomfortably hot. Both Lucas and I were dressed in the shirts and pants we'd gotten from Camellia, and now we turned our long pants into shorts, rolled up the sleeves of our shirts, and zipped the mesh side vents open. I was beginning to see why people bought this kind of stuff instead of just going to Target and getting jeans and T-shirts. I was almost beginning to wish we'd packed the pith helmets with the personal cooling systems. They were still back in Minnesota.

Instead of the green grass and trees we'd seen coming out of the city, the plants here were low bushes, yellowish grass either tall or short, and, every so often, a tree shaped like an umbrella that I'd seen on nature programs before. Bernard said the trees were acacias. The sky seemed enormous, bright blue and stretching from flat horizon to flat horizon. It was like I'd never seen so much sky.

We'd been driving in the valley only a few miles when we saw a spot of red behind a string of cattle. The red turned out to be a very tall, very thin young guy wrapped in a red cloth and carrying a huge stick.

"It's somebody from the Maasai tribe!" Lucas said, her voice totally excited. "Wow, this is awesome!"

A few minutes later, Bernard slowed the van for a pit stop at a place where Kenyan people were selling beautiful carvings and masks and jewelry, along with snacks and soft drinks. Before we looked at or bought anything, Lucas and I headed for the bathrooms. I had my eyes on the ground where the two brightest blue birds I'd ever seen were fighting over some crumbs.

Lucas, ahead of me, said, "Holy schmack, look at that," and slowed down so much that I ran right into her.

The signs for the women's and men's were big paintings on the wall outside the bathrooms: a warrior with a spear for the men's, and—this is what Lucas was talking about—a woman naked to the waist for the women's.

"We sure don't have that in Minnesota," I said, and we both got the giggles.

5

The Omen

When we were back in the van, I said, "Bernard, we know that *jambo* means *hello* from watching *The Lion King*. But what does *safari* mean?"

"It means *journey* in Swahili."

"Cool!" I said. "So we're already on safari!"

He nodded. "Right you are."

It wasn't more than about five minutes later that Bernard casually said, "Look at that field on your right."

"Giraffes!" I said. There they were. Seven giraffes walking in a line so close to us I could see their spots.

Lucas and I yelled together, "We don't have that in Minnesota!" My heart was pumping really hard. We'd just seen the first real African animals of our trip.

I'd been to zoos and I'd seen probably hundreds of shows about animals on the Nature Channel or PBS, but when you're really there with them, watching them out in the open for the first time, it's completely different.

Both Lucas and I kept looking at the giraffes even after we passed them, turning around in our seats. "Wow! I didn't expect to see animals *outside* the game park," I said.

"It is likely we will see many animals between here and the Mara," Bernard said. "In fact, look up ahead on the right side of the road."

"Baboons!" Lucas said.

"This is so sweet I can't believe it!" I added.

A bunch of them were sitting there, big circles of gray fur around their faces, some of them with their arms around cute little baby baboons.

We stopped for Lucas to take photos. When we started up again, I said, "We were so close, I'll bet I could have hit one of them if I'd thrown a gum wrapper out the window! Not that I would, but you know what I mean."

Next we saw three ostriches running through a field, their white heads held high over their black bodies.

A few miles later, Bernard pointed off to our left. "Look, Lucas. There is your first Maasai village."

It was a collection of maybe a dozen mud huts surrounded by a wall of branches.

Lucas pulled out her camera, but Bernard cautioned her. "I should tell you, Miss Lucas, that taking a picture without the people's permission can be seen as an invasion of privacy. Especially in the Maasai culture."

"I suppose that makes sense," Lucas said. "I don't think I would want somebody from another country visiting Saint Paul and sticking a camera in my face."

I thought about when Mom and I had visited the Indian reservation in South Dakota. She'd told me we couldn't take any pictures at all because it would be disrespectful.

"Do you see that town up ahead?" Bernard asked.

"Yes, I see the outline at the horizon," I answered.

"That's Narok, the village my family comes from. It is a small town in the heart of Maasai country. Many Maasai live there, but the population is made up of people from many tribes. My family is Kikuyu. Sometimes tourists stop at Narok to take photographs of the people of the village, and I can tell you, the villagers find it very strange."

"That's probably not the only thing they find strange about the tourists," Lucas said.

Bernard looked into the rearview mirror, his eyes crinkling in a big smile. "You are right about that, Miss Lucas. Western tourists seem as strange to the people in the villages as the village residents seem to the Western tourists."

"Does your family still live in Narok?" I asked.

"My sister and her husband still live there, and they have several children who are in school. My family—my wife and my children—live in Nairobi now. All except for my daughter, Anyango, who you will meet at the lodge where you will be staying. She wishes to make a career in the tourist industry, so she works in the kitchen and as a waitress at the lodge. You will see her tonight. Professor Wanjohi and the others from the archaeological site all have their own table in the dining room, and Anyango is their waitress at dinner."

"How old is she?" I asked.

"She is sixteen. She is a good girl."

You could tell Bernard was proud of his daughter, because this whole time his face had been beaming.

Narok itself was a small but busy town with a lot of businesses along the way, and stands selling what looked like delicious fruits and vegetables. What made it different from the other places we'd driven through was all the Maasai people on the streets—tall, many of the men in red or orange, the young ones with long hair, and the women, in colors that weren't red, with hair cut close to their head.

"Look at the schoolchildren. They just got out of class for the day," Bernard said. Sure enough, dozens of little school kids were running down a sidewalk, laughing and chasing each other like kids do. They were dressed in pink and gray uniforms.

"Cute!" Lucas said.

"Yes, the people here are poor, but the children are happy," Bernard said.

Outside of Narok, we were back in the African countryside again. The first animals we saw were a herd of impala. They're a kind of antelope that have these long horns that go up and curve back, like beautifully shaped, pointy handlebars.

After that there were the Thomson's gazelles, another kind of antelope, which Bernard called Tommies. They were beautiful, with a dark stripe down their sides. But it was when we saw the zebras that I got really excited. They were right by the side of the road, hundreds and hundreds of them, all grazing together, one big herd.

Lucas said, "Wow! Cool! This is even better than I ever thought it would be!"

"Zebras!" I said. "We're driving along looking out the window at a field full of zebras!"

Bernard smiled into the rearview mirror. "No zebras in Minnesota?"

We just smiled back.

It wasn't long after the zebras that the van suddenly slowed and Bernard said, "Is either of you young ladies afraid of snakes?"

"Nope," we both said. Lucas's big phobia is spiders, and mine is heights.

"Well then, you might want to get out of your seats and look."

The van pulled to the side of the road, and we stood up under the raised roof.

Ahead of us an enormously long, dark-gray snake slithered across the pavement.

"That's a spitting cobra," Bernard said. "One of the deadliest snakes in the world."

"It must be two yards long!" I said. I heard Lucas's camera clicking beside me.

"I believe it is longer than that. Perhaps over eight feet," Bernard said. "He sees us now. Watch his head."

The snake had stopped, its body coiled. Slowly the head rose, and I saw that hood cobras have. I felt the hair on the back of my neck stand up.

Lucas, camera down now, asked in a small voice, "How far can they spit?"

"Several meters. Or yards, as you would say in America. Do not worry, I have kept you a safe distance away. And you will notice that the motor is running." During this whole answer, Bernard had never taken his eyes off the snake.

Just then the cobra's head lunged forward. Venom flew through the air, landing a few feet in front of the van.

"That was attempted murder!" I said. (I watch a lot of cop shows.)

Bernard nodded. "Yes, and now that has failed, it is going off to other things."

We watched as the snake writhed its way over the rest of the pavement and onto the dry ground, leaving its loopy track in the dust.

I flopped down in my seat and let out my breath in a whoosh, my heart pounding in my ears.

"Wow!" Lucas said. "That's the biggest and baddest snake I've ever seen!"

Bernard nodded and smiled at us in the rearview mirror, then put the van in gear and pulled onto the highway. "The spitting cobra is about as big and as bad as snakes come, Lucas."

I thought about the big bad snake for a while, pulled out my diary to write about it, but found it was too bumpy to write anything. It had been really exciting to see it on our first day.

It never occurred to me that the snake could be an omen.

6

Not the Kind of Tents We'd Expected

Only a few minutes later we got to the entrance of the Masai Mara Game Reserve and headed into it on a gravel road. We were still in the Rift Valley, but the countryside looked different. Instead of just a big, dry, flat field with bushes and a few acacia trees sticking up, like it had been pretty much since we got down into the valley, it was now a mixture of hills and plains, with greener grass and lots more trees, bigger bushes, and even a little stream here and there.

Bernard pulled a cell phone out of his pocket. "I will call to let your uncle know we made it safely. He will not be able to receive the call in the dig site itself, but I will leave a message."

"Tell him *hi*, and that we're having a wonderful time," I said.

When he was finished with the call, Lucas said, "Does everybody here have cell phones?"

Bernard smiled in the rearview mirror. "Almost. Mobile phones, as we call them, have allowed people here to be in touch as never before. They're the only phones most people have outside the main cities. Even many of the Maasai herders have mobiles."

Bernard made another call, and the next minute we pulled off the highway and down a short drive into the parking lot of our safari camp. The sidewalk led up the hill and around to the front of the lodge building, which was wood and stone. On the far side there was an open-air bar, and closer to the front, a patio with tables. Bright, flowering plants grew all around.

In the lobby, two staff members waited to greet us with warm, rolled-up washcloths and glasses of cool mango juice. It was wonderful to be able to wipe our faces and hands with the damp cloths. The juice tasted delicious. I decided right away that I was addicted to mango juice.

After Bernard told the desk clerk who we were, a friendly young African guy, maybe seventeen or eighteen years old, led Lucas and me from the big wooden lodge down a gentle slope lined with low flowering plants to our tents, wheeling a dolly with our bags on it. He wore a green African print tunic and green pants, and his name tag said SAM.

We had known we would be staying in a tent camp. We'd thought it would be like one of the Minnesota state parks, with tents here and there and a big shared bathroom and shower building. Or maybe it would have rows of side-by-side tents with a shared bathroom.

This was nothing like that. These tents were huge, and so tall that an adult could stand up in them. They were all separate from each other, scattered around the grounds, which were full of flowers and trees. Charlie had told Uncle Geoff that we should all bring our swimsuits because there was a pool, and it turned out to be a really nice one. In fact the whole place totally rocked.

The tent where Lucas and I would be staying was only the second one in a winding row of tents along the path we were on. Sam unzipped the entrance flap and we all stepped in. The space inside was as big as a regular motel room, and it had a floor made of concrete. Sam went to each of our beds, turning on the bedside lamps.

"This is amazing!" Lucas said. "I never thought we'd have electric lights in our tent!"

Then Sam walked to the back wall, which was made of canvas, and pulled aside a flap. "This is your toilet, ladies," he said politely.

Lucas and I peeked inside. It was a whole room at the back of the tent, a complete bathroom with a toilet and sink and a big shower.

"A bathroom in a tent!" I said. "It's just like a motel room, but cooler."

"It's awesome," Lucas added.

"There are bottles of water on your bedside tables,

and two bottles of water in the bathroom. These are for drinking. Please use the tap water for washing only. If you drink it, it can make you very ill."

Sam arranged our bags on the luggage racks, told us dinner would be served at seven, then said good-bye, taking the tip Lucas gave him.

When he was gone, I let a minute pass, then said, "Do you realize, we are now officially on our own? No Mom. No Uncle Geoff."

"No Fair Camellia. No Allen the Meep. Not even the Brat Child."

"Alone in the tent. And this is the way it's going to stay!"

"I hope Uncle Geoff doesn't stick his nose too much into our business."

"Especially now that we have a mystery to solve."

"This place is pretty cool, isn't it?" I said a few minutes later, flip-flopping beside Lucas on the sidewalk on our way to the pool. The path led through shrubs on both sides with big, bright flowers, and the air smelled heavenly.

Lucas took a long sniff. "It's gorgeous. It's so wonderful after Minnesota in December. Not that I don't like snow, but it's great to feel warm and be around these plants and flowers that smell so good."

We walked for a second in silence. Except for a few guys in the bar, the lodge seemed to be deserted at this time of day, and it was sweet feeling like we had it to ourselves. I thought about the group still out at the dig.

"Um, Lucas."

"Ye-e-e-s?"

"About the looting."

"What about it?"

"Well, I was thinking kind of two different things. One is that it would be fun to see if we could solve the mystery."

Lucas looked at me as if I was a little nuts. "I thought that was, like, obvious."

The pool was kidney shaped. I led the way around to the other side where we could get the most sun.

"Well, it might seem obvious to you, but I was also thinking that we probably can't do it. I mean, how would we even start?"

"I think step one is to pay a visit to the Simba Hill cave. I hope we can go soon. It isn't *exactly* the scene of the crime, but it's as close as we can get. Maybe if we see it, we'll get a better idea of what the criminals did exactly. Digging artifacts up and everything."

I heaved a secret sigh of relief as I pulled a lounge chair around to face the sun. I'd been worried that Lucas wouldn't want to go out to the cave, because I knew she wasn't as interested in archaeology as I was. But now she was going to be looking at it as, like, a detective.

"I'm not saying visiting the scene of the crime won't

be helpful," I said, stepping out of my flip-flops. The concrete was warm, almost hot under my feet. "What I'm worried about is that the bad guy, or bad guys, or bad woman or whoever, could be anybody from around here. It could be somebody from one of the villages outside the Masai Mara. Or it could be somebody from another one of the lodges in the game reserve. . . ." I made a gesture with my hand and let my voice trail off to give an idea of all the ways we might be meeped on this.

"All we need is a toehold in the rock." Lucas scooted a chair up next to mine and pulled off the T-shirt she wore over her swimsuit.

I sat down at the side of the pool and dangled my legs in the cool water. "What exactly is that supposed to mean?"

Lucas had taken one single daylong class in rock climbing at REI during the summer, and ever since then she'd been fantasizing about getting to be really good at it. I was dreading spring, when she was signed up to take a longer course. I would have bet any money that rock climbing would be her next big obsession.

"It just means you have to have a place to start," she said, and threw her T-shirt onto her chair.

I rolled my eyes and said, "And that would be . . . ?"

"Just one single clue."

I didn't say anything.

"Don't worry, Kari. We've solved mysteries before. We'll solve this one, too."

She walked around to the diving board and dove into the water.

That was another thing about Lucas: she always thought the two of us could do anything, and she was brave enough to *try* anything. I called her Lucas the Lionheart. Just then I wasn't exactly sure if this was a good quality or a bad one.

7

Anyango Means Friend

The water felt wonderful. We both took a long swim, then lay out on our lounge chairs, smelling the chlorine and the flowers and soaking up the sun. At one point, this incredibly cute little animal ran out of the bushes. It looked exactly like an antelope, complete with horns and hooves, but it was not much bigger than a toy poodle. It scooted along the side of the pool, then disappeared back into the bushes.

"That was seriously one of the cutest animals I've ever seen," I said.

"I think it's called a dik-dik," Lucas said.

Turned out, that was the only fact that Lucas let drop pretty much that whole afternoon. Her resolution not to pelt me with mini-lectures seemed to be working.

Eventually, both of us got bored sunbathing. I pulled out my journal and Lucas got out her art pad and started a detailed drawing of a baboon like the ones we'd seen that morning. I was sitting where I could see what she was doing. I was always amazed to watch how good she was, and how perfectly she remembered whatever she was working on.

I think I'm pretty good at painting and working with pastels, and one of the things I wanted to do when I got home where I had my art stuff was to try some pictures of African places and animals. I wouldn't be able to do it from memory, though. I'd have to work from the photos Lucas was taking because I don't remember everything I've seen the way she does.

I was busy writing in my journal about our trip so far when a shadow fell across the page and a voice in front of me said, "Would you like to order something cool to drink?"

It was a young woman wearing the same kind of green tunic and pants that Sam had worn when he took us to our tent. She was maybe a couple of years older than Lucas and I, very slender, and had an intelligent look in her dark eyes.

Lucas ordered a Coke, and I ordered mango juice.

When she'd gone, Lucas said, "Did you notice her name badge? Her name is Anya."

It took me a second to think what she was talking about. Then I said, "Oh, like maybe she could be Bernard's daughter Anyango. Is that what you're saying?"

Lucas nodded. "We'll have to ask her. Since she works here, I wonder if she's heard any gossip about who might have taken the artifacts."

I nodded. "I'll bet there are a lot of rumors."

"Let's pump her for info when she comes back!" Lucas was obviously all enthused.

I didn't like this word *pump*. "I think we'd better at least be polite about it. Not make her think that we're using her or anything."

"Okay, you go first," she said. Lucas is better at the lionheart kind of thing, but most of the time I'm better at being subtle.

So when Anya came back a few minutes later and put our drinks on the little table between us, I asked, "How do you say *thank you* in Swahili?"

"It is *asante sana*," she answered.

"*Asante sana* then," I said. "I like your name. Anya. It's really pretty."

"Thank you," she said, and added, "*Asante sana*." She smiled without opening her mouth, letting her eyes do most of the smiling for her. She wasn't exactly pretty, but when she smiled like that and her cheeks bunched up, she looked really cute.

Lucas gave her money for the drinks and a tip.

"Are you Anyango, Bernard's daughter?" I asked.

Her smile got bigger, this time showing her bright, white teeth. "Yes, Bernard is my father."

"Bernard is an awesome guy!" I said, and Lucas added, "Yes, we both really like him."

"*Everyone* seems to like him," I said.

"My father is a wonderful man." It wasn't that she didn't sound like she believed it—I was sure she thought her father was wonderful—but somehow she didn't sound as happy or enthused about it as I would have thought she would.

I thought maybe I should change the subject. "Anyango is a beautiful name. I like it better than the regular English names a lot of the other people have around here. Like Sam, the guy who carried our bags when we arrived."

Anya smiled with her eyes again. "Sam is just his Christian name. He is also called Khamisi. It means he was born on a Thursday."

This was a new idea to me, a name that meant you were born on a certain day.

"What does Anyango mean?" Lucas asked.

"Anyango means friend."

"A name that means *friend*, that's very cool," I said. "Is Bernard your father's only name, or is it just his Christian name?"

"My father's Kenyan name is Jelani."

"What does that mean?"

"It means great or powerful."

"Your dad said that you want someday to make your career in the tourist business," Lucas said.

Anya nodded. "Yes. Many people here in Kenya who work with tourists can make a very good living, and it is an industry in which there are more and more women. Women are very strong in our society, you know. Only a few years ago, a Kenyan woman won the Nobel Peace Prize."

Lucas nodded. "Wangari Maathai. For planting all those trees." She would know.

Anya, clearly proud that a woman from her country had won such an absolutely big deal honor, raised her head and said, "Yes, she's responsible for an organization that has planted many millions of trees, and helped save the ecology of Kenya and other countries. She is just one of many strong Kenyan women. I want to be a strong Kenyan woman, and perhaps have my own guesthouse or restaurant. Or maybe I could manage a hotel."

"That's awesome," I said. "I want to be an archaeologist when I grow up, and Lucas wants to be an environmental lawyer."

"Yeah, maybe I can work with Wangari Maathai," Lucas added.

Anya said, "We are from different sides of the world, but we all have our dreams of doing big things."

I'd backtracked a little getting to know more about Anya, but we still needed to find out if she knew any good gossip about the looting at the Simba Hill site.

"It must be nice that your dad can come see you when

he's here. He's been working for the Simba Hill dig crew for a long time, hasn't he?"

"Yes, it has been almost a year."

"We found out today that someone was trying to smuggle some of the artifacts from the site out of the country," I said.

Anya nodded, but the smile and confident look that had been there before disappeared from her face. She was holding the tray in both her hands, and I noticed that her fingers started moving, as if she might be nervous. I wondered if maybe she had to get back to work.

I made the mistake of looking at Lucas. She must have thought I meant it was her turn to talk, because she said, "I know this story was only in the newspaper this morning, but do the people here at the lodge have any ideas who might be taking the rock art from the cave?"

Anya looked down at the ground. "I have heard . . . there are some people . . ." She hesitated, then looked up again. "Perhaps you should talk with Sam." Just then someone called "Anyango," followed by a bunch of words I didn't understand. I turned around and saw a guy with a lodge uniform coming toward us. He didn't look mean, but he was obviously telling Anya to come back to the lodge.

"I must go now and help prepare for new guests." She turned and started down the path.

"When could we talk to Sam?" I asked after her,

but she kept walking quickly toward the lodge.

"What do you think that was about?" Lucas asked when she was gone.

"I don't have a clue. Maybe it's about somebody suspected of doing the smuggling."

Lucas turned and looked at me. "But who could they suspect that would make Anya so nervous?"

8

Maria's Suspicions

Uncle Geoff stopped at our tent on his way back from the dig site.

"Isn't this place amazing?" he asked. "I had no idea it was going to be quite so fancy. I guess the archaeological crew got a group rate, since there were a lot of them and they were going to be here most of the year." He looked at me. "Don't get the wrong idea about archaeological digs. Believe me, kiddo, it's usually not this plush."

"The pool is awesome," I said. "We tried it this afternoon. Oh, and by the way, while we were there we met Bernard's daughter, Anya. She's cool. Really smart, and nice, like her dad. Bernard said she'd be our waitress at dinner."

"I hope we get to know her better," Lucas said. I noticed she didn't say anything about those last, kind of weird minutes with Anya, and I decided not to say anything either.

"Great! Maybe you'll make a new friend while you're here," Uncle Geoff said. "And speaking of the pool, I might take a quick plunge. I guess Charlie and I are just two tents down, so give a holler if you need anything."

He looked from one of us to the other. "Um, you guys are going to be on your own a lot here."

I wanted to say, "The point of that being . . ." Instead I just stood there and tried to look all grown-up and responsible so he wouldn't think he had to stick his nose into what Lucas and I were doing. Especially now that we had a mystery to solve.

He obviously couldn't come up with the right thing to say next, so Lucas piped up. "I wouldn't worry about us too much," she said. "We're going to be in this fenced-in lodge at night, and in the daytime, Bernard will be with us, and everybody agrees that he's, like, a saint or something. I don't think we can get into a whole lot of trouble."

"Okay," Uncle Geoff said, still hesitating. "I guess I'll go and get suited up. What are you guys going to do?"

"We were just about to get dressed for dinner, even though it's a little early," I said. "We want to send some e-mails from the lodge."

"Okay. Wait for me in the lobby and we'll go to the dining room together," Uncle Geoff said, and off he went.

We dressed in skirts because Charlie had told Uncle Geoff in one of his messages that people dressed up for the evening meal. When we were ready, we went up to the computer bank set up for guests to use. Lucas sent a message to her parents, and I sent one to Mom telling her about the animals we'd seen and how excited I was that Professor Wanjohi said we could visit the dig site while we were here. I'd told her about the smuggling in the e-mail I sent when we were still at the hotel in Nairobi. Now I said we didn't know anything more than I'd said then.

Uncle Geoff met us at the door to the dining room at seven o'clock, and a staff member led us to a big table reserved for our whole group. The others were already there: the professor, Charlie, and a woman we'd never seen before.

When we got to the table, both the professor and Charlie stood up to greet us. As we sat down, Professor Wanjohi said, "Maria, this is Geoff's niece, Kari, and her friend Lucas.

"Girls," the professor continued, "I'd like you to meet Maria Ketteridge. She's from South Africa and works in my department at the university. She specializes in the cultural aspects of the site. What the people who lived here did, religious traditions, family structure, et cetera."

I noticed as we shook hands that Maria had fashionable short black hair and dark eyes. Her smooth skin was just dark enough that I thought she probably had some grandparent or great-grandparent who was black. She was pretty, even though she was at least as old as Uncle Geoff and Mom.

She smiled while she said hello, turned to Uncle Geoff, and patted the chair beside hers. "Geoff, I saved a place for you."

I glanced at Lucas and raised my eyebrows, and she gave me the tiniest nod.

I happened to look at Charlie, who was sitting on the other side of Maria. He winked at me, and although he didn't exactly smile, his mustache definitely twitched. It made me want to laugh, and it also made me think that Maria's flirting had started earlier in the day.

I've never described Uncle Geoff very much, because he's my uncle and I don't really think about his looks. He's not exactly a fashion model, but he's good looking enough that he's never had any trouble finding girlfriends. His black, curly hair is cut pretty short and sticks up around his head in a way that looks good on him. He works out, so he's fit. And he has nice, even teeth, and a straight nose. Now, as I watched him sitting down in his sport coat and open-neck shirt over black jeans, I thought it wasn't surprising that a pretty woman like Maria, who was about his age, would find him attractive.

Uncle Geoff acted like he didn't notice anything special about how Maria was looking at him. I've noticed that guys often seem like they don't have a clue about flirting. I wondered if he was putting on an act or not.

A minute later, Anya came to pour the water and take our drinks order. She started with the professor, who was at the head of the table. When he was finished, he smiled and said thank you and Anya smiled back. Lucas and I were next, and we did the same thing. This happened when she got to Maria, too, but the smile Anya gave then looked like she was forcing herself to do it, and she had a wary expression in her dark eyes before she moved on to Uncle Geoff and Charlie.

Nobody else at the table seemed to notice, or if they did, they were ignoring it. I wondered what was up.

The lodge served all its meals buffet style, and the whole huge front section of the dining room was devoted to food. There was practically everything you could think of to eat: salads, main dishes, cheeses, breads, fruits, and a whole section devoted to delicious looking desserts.

"There must be some big deal between Anya and Maria about who did the smuggling," I muttered to Lucas as we went to pick out our salads. "I wish we knew who Maria thought was guilty."

"We'll find out," Lucas said as she picked up a plate.

"How do you know?"

"I'll ask her."

When we got back to the table, the professor kept the promise he had made in Nairobi and asked us all about our trip out that day, and the things we'd seen that had been different from home. We told him about some of our We Don't Have That in Minnesota moments, including the topless woman painted on the side of the bathroom, which made him chuckle.

We finished our salads and Anya came again to pick up our empty plates. The scene went exactly the same as it had before, with her looking cautious, almost unfriendly, when she got close to Maria.

When we got back from choosing our main courses, the professor looked at Lucas and me and said, "When are you going to come out and join us at the dig site?"

"Could we—" I broke off and glanced at Lucas. "Could we go there tomorrow? Seeing people actually working in an archaeological site would be *so awesome!*"

"Yeah, and I'd kind of like to see the place where the smuggled rocks came from. Or, I mean, not exactly, but close to where they came from."

It was almost like, for a little while, the archaeologists had forgotten about the theft of the artifacts, because suddenly all four of them got the same grim look on their faces.

There was a long silence. Then Charlie said, "In a suitcase! They smuggled those prehistoric treasures out in a *suitcase.*" His nostrils flared and his eyes narrowed. You could tell he was really mad just thinking about it.

About that time we finished our main courses and Professor Wanjohi excused himself from the table and said he had to go back and work on an article he was writing.

The minute he was gone, Lucas gave me A Look, turned to Maria, and said, "So, Maria, who do *you* think stole the rock art?"

Most kids who are brought up in Minnesota are too polite to ask a grown-up a question like that. I'd never have enough nerve to do it. Of course, Lucas always has enough nerve to do anything.

Maria batted her eyelashes for a second, glanced up at Uncle Geoff, and said, "I shouldn't say anything about it. It's a rather sensitive situation and I'm sure the professor wouldn't be best pleased."

"I'd actually like to know myself who you think might be the culprit," Uncle Geoff said.

Maria gave this little laugh that was obviously meant to sound cute and tinkly but was really just annoying. "Well, if you insist, I think the most likely thief is Bernard."

I sucked in my breath, and Uncle Geoff's eyebrows shot up in surprise.

"You're kidding," Lucas said. It was something I wouldn't have expected Lucas to say, and it showed just how surprised she was.

"I know he came highly recommended, but he's the most logical suspect," Maria continued.

She must have noticed our astonished looks, because

she said, "I'm not alone in this! Since the news broke this morning, I've heard from several people who agree with me."

What people? I wondered. Who had she been talking to since this morning?

"He was Professor Wanjohi's driver during the earliest phase of the dig, before the rest of us came out," she continued. "I believe that during that time, perhaps when the professor was in Nairobi or when he came back to Johannesburg to get the team assembled, Bernard and his brother-in-law found another entrance to the cave, and they've probably been taking artifacts out ever since. You may not know that his sister's husband is a known thief, and has been imprisoned on more than one occasion."

For the first time in my life, I understood the expression, *You could have knocked me over with a feather*. The whole idea of Bernard being a criminal was so surprising to me that I felt I could almost keel over in my chair.

Charlie must have seen how surprised I looked, because he peered at me over his glasses. "Maria has a suspicious nature," he said. "I don't believe Bernard is the thief."

Maria gave Charlie a dirty look, and said, "Well, a great many people around here agree with me."

"I wouldn't say a great many agree, Maria," Charlie said. He had his usual easygoing expression, but his voice had tension in it. "I don't think the news has been around long enough for *many* people to have made up their minds about who's involved. My guess is that by the time the story is widely known, most of the people who know Bernard well will be convinced he's *not* guilty, no matter what his brother-in-law may have done in the past. He's a terrific guy."

"I'll admit, he puts on a good show," Maria said to Charlie, then turned to Uncle Geoff, totally ignoring Lucas and me.

"Bernard has a big, extended family to support. With the unemployment rate over thirty percent, a majority of the people who have jobs around here are supporting not just their own children, but their parents, and the families of their brothers and sisters. That's enough of a reason for him to try to make a bit of money on the side."

"Just as good a reason why he wouldn't want to threaten a good job by becoming involved in smuggling," Charlie responded.

"But how about the guard?" Uncle Geoff said, as if partly to get everybody's mind off the disagreement between Maria and Charlie. "Or is there more than one?"

"Right now, with Bernard doing the driving for Kari and Lucas, there's only one guard," Charlie said. "Prosper, the one you met today, Geoff."

Charlie looked at Lucas and me and gestured with his head toward a table in the corner. "He's sitting with the safari guides. He's the one with the hat."

Prosper was a big guy, tall, a little overweight, with broad shoulders. And yes, even at dinner, he was wearing a hat. It was shaped like a cowboy hat made out of brown leather, with the brim slightly curled up on one side.

"Up until now, Prosper and Bernard have made sure all the daylight hours are covered," Charlie said. "For the most part, Prosper takes the morning shift and Bernard has taken the afternoon, but Bernard has also done some other driving, like taking us to and from the airfield. The professor has just hired someone to serve as a second guard until Bernard is free again. It's a member of the staff here at the lodge who wanted to earn a little extra money."

"How about at night?" Uncle Geoff asked.

"The lions manage the night shift," Maria said. "That's why they call it Simba Hill. Anyone who came after dark would end up as prey."

Lucas and I looked at each other, and I shivered. Lion prey.

"Not a happy thought," Uncle Geoff said.

There were a few seconds of silence, and as if he'd been waiting to change the subject, Charlie said, "Anyone besides me up for choosing some desserts?"

9

TMI about Maria

"I do *not* believe Bernard is the thief," Lucas muttered to me as she picked out a small dish of chocolate mousse.

I decided to try the sweet potato pudding with coconut, which was labeled a local dessert. "No meeping kidding," I said.

I would have said more, but Maria appeared at my side, pointed out the pudding I'd taken a dish of, and told Uncle Geoff he should try it. "Of course, I can't have any. Too many calories," she added, and laughed that tinkly laugh.

If she was hoping Uncle Geoff would say something about her figure, which I have to admit was pretty good, she was disappointed. Instead, he shook his head. "Afraid I'll pass. Never been crazy about coconut." He took a piece of pear almond cake.

When everybody got back to the table, their plates

loaded down with goodies, the time for talking about the smuggling was obviously over. This gave Maria a chance to talk about herself, which she did, completely hogging the conversation.

She started off talking about some of the interesting work she had done at archaeological sites over the years. She was very careful to give a lot of credit to Professor Wanjohi and to talk about how honored she was to be chosen to be part of his team. In fact, she'd been talking for probably five minutes or so before I realized that everything she said just happened to make her look good.

Like, she was talking about a consulting job she'd done for some South African museum, and somehow she fit in the fact that the person who hired her had been in her college at Oxford, and they had both taken firsts, which I figured meant they'd gotten really good grades. She described a show about the connections between modern and prehistoric art that she'd helped put together at the Tate Britain, a famous museum in London.

The worst bragging was when she said, "I think the most interesting dig I was ever involved with was when one of Mary Leakey's protégés at Olduvai Gorge contacted me, and I worked with them for a season."

With a quick look in Uncle Geoff's direction, she added, "I can't imagine why they wanted *me*." Tinkle tinkle. "At that point in my career I'd had a great deal less experience than I do today."

Lucas nudged me with her elbow to show how she felt. She knew—and I'd learned in getting ready for the trip—that Olduvai Gorge in Tanzania was one of the most important archaeological sites in the world, where they found a lot of traces of prehistoric humans. Mary Leakey was an incredibly famous scientist who headed the dig. So this was big-time showing off, which I suppose she thought would really impress an archaeologist like Uncle Geoff.

But one time, when Maria wasn't looking at him and the other people at the table were looking at *her*, Uncle Geoff crossed his eyes at me as if he meant to say, "Can you believe this?" I almost burst out laughing.

Charlie kept quiet, although a couple of times, like when she mentioned Mary Leakey, his mustache definitely twitched, and he looked out at Maria over his round glasses.

Finally, after she'd been talking for at least fifteen minutes, she stopped long enough to sip her coffee, which gave Charlie and Lucas and me a chance to go get seconds on desserts. Uncle Geoff, realizing he was going to be alone at the table with Maria, decided it was time for a trip to the men's room.

When we got to the buffet area, Lucas said to Charlie, "Does Maria talk about herself *all* the time?"

He looked at us over his glasses. "I predict you'll leave Africa knowing quite a lot about Maria."

As we ate our desserts, Anya went around the table refilling coffee cups. Charlie was telling a story about a time he had dug up the bones of a cow thinking it was a dinosaur fossil. I'm sure it was funny, and even funnier because of the way he told it, but I didn't catch all of what he was saying because of an expression on Anya's face that hadn't been there before: Fear. Worry. Something like that.

She walked around the table doing the refilling like she was a robot. When someone smiled at her, she didn't smile back. And she didn't treat Maria differently from anybody else.

Something very wrong was going on. If all eyes hadn't been on Charlie, I'm sure others would have noticed it, but as it was, I seemed to be the only one clued in.

While everybody was laughing at Charlie's joke, a folded note landed in my lap. I made sure no one was looking before I opened it up. It said, *Sam and I will meet you at 22:00 hours in front of the candelabra trees.*

That meant ten o'clock the way we tell time in America.

I looked at Uncle Geoff, who was saying something to Lucas—neither of them seemed to notice what was going on with Anya—then looked at my watch. It was almost nine.

If I'd been right about Anya's expression, this note meant that she and maybe Bernard needed help. I really,

really wanted to help both of them, and I knew Lucas would, too. But how were we supposed to sneak away and meet somebody at ten o'clock? And what and where were the candelabra trees?

We'd just have to figure it all out.

10

First Appearance of the Ghost of Mom

Maria excused herself after dessert because she said she had to send an e-mail, and Uncle Geoff and Charlie headed to the bar for a nightcap.

We asked the desk clerk about the candelabra trees, and she said they were all the way at the end of the path that went past our tent, and we shouldn't touch them because they were dangerous. Before she could explain further, somebody else came up to the desk and she turned away from us.

Lucas looked at me, shrugged, and raised her eyebrows.

"What*ever*," I said, shooting a look at the desk clerk. Obviously, we were going to have to find out about the candelabra trees for ourselves.

We started down the path, still close enough to the lodge that the laughing and talking from the people at the outdoor bar almost drowned out the crickets, and the light from the building was brighter than the glow from the small ankle-height lamps along the way.

The path led across a wooden bridge over a small pond. The bridge had a porch-like place halfway across it built off to the side, with a roof and a bench that stuck out over the water. We stopped and sat down. I knew we'd be safe for a least a few minutes while Uncle Geoff and Charlie hung out.

Sitting there, we were surrounded by night sounds: crickets, a few birds still calling, people's voices at the open-air bar, and an animal sound, like a grunt, from far away. A couple walked across the bridge just as we sat down, so we were quiet until they passed.

I had shown Lucas the note when we were still in the dining room. Now, lowering my voice—I didn't know who was around, and besides, voices carry a long way over water—I told her about how Anya had looked when she went around the table that last time.

"But you don't know what was wrong?" she asked.

I just raised my eyebrows and looked at her.

"Okay, okay, how would you know?" We were both quiet for a while, then she whispered, "Are you sure we're right about Bernard? That he wouldn't be the smuggler, I mean?"

I should probably explain about this. Like I've said before, Lucas is really, really smart. I do pretty well at school, but she's way smarter than I am. She's smarter than almost anybody. I never feel stupid around her, though, because both of us know that there are things I'm better at than she is. And one of those things is figuring out people.

Usually it doesn't take me long to get a pretty good idea of what somebody's like—whether they're nice, whether I'd trust them or wouldn't. Sometimes I'm wrong, but not very often. Mom's like that, too. She says it's part of being intuitive, which we both are. Smart as Lucas is, she's not intuitive.

"Are you kidding?" I said, answering Lucas's question. "He's a totally nice guy! And remember what the professor said about Bernard having been his driver for the last ten years? A guy like Bernard isn't going to be a thief."

"Well, that's what I thought. I mean, that it couldn't be him. I'm glad it isn't just me who feels that way."

"I wish we could find out who really did it. Prove Bernard is innocent, I mean."

Lucas said, "Well, we might as well get started. I think Little Miss Wonderful did it."

"You mean Maria, Miss Tinkly Laugh? You think she's in on the smuggling?"

"Mm-hmm. I think she was accusing Bernard so nobody thinks she was the one who did it."

"Why do you think she's guilty?"

"Because she's obnoxious."

"But being obnoxious doesn't mean you're a criminal!"

"I suppose you're right." Lucas heaved a huge sigh, as if she was sorry to have to admit it. "At least your uncle isn't as impressed with her as she wanted him to be."

"No meeping kidding. You missed the time he crossed his eyes at me in the middle of something she was saying."

She smiled. "Crossed his eyes, huh? I wish I'd seen that."

"Yeah, I definitely have the feeling that he and Maria won't end up together living happily ever after."

I heard the sound of footsteps and looked down the path. "Guess who?" I breathed.

"Little Miss Wonderful?"

"Right on the first try. I don't think she's close enough to hear us, but we should probably be safe and talk about something else."

I raised my voice to what I hoped was something like normal. "Weren't those animals we saw today awesome?"

"I can't wait to get out for our first real safari drive!"

We said a few more things about the animals, waited until she was almost out of sight down the path, then started to our tent.

"I hope Uncle Geoff doesn't find out where we're going. I don't suppose he'd want us to be walking around this late, even if it's safe because of the wall around the compound."

That was when what I came to think of as the Ghost of Mom came to me for the first time. I could see her standing beside us with her hands on her hips, glaring. I was pretty sure she'd tie us to our beds if she knew what we were planning to do.

Lucas looked at her watch. "It's nine thirty. Why don't we turn off all our lights, zip everything up, and go down to the candelabra trees now? That way, when your uncle passes our tent, he'll think we've knocked off for the night."

"Good thinking," I said.

"Thanks. I thought so."

I unzipped the tent, went in, and looked out the mesh window as Maria continued down the pathway. "Whew. She's passed."

"I could imagine her following us in here and making us listen to stories about how important she is," Lucas said, rummaging around for the flashlight, which she had in her suitcase.

"You mean about how Bono proposed to her the last time he visited South Africa?"

"Yes, and she wouldn't want us to leave Kenya without knowing that Bill and Melinda Gates asked her to guide the scientists in creating a cure for malaria."

I turned off the bedside light and Lucas flipped on the flashlight, opened the flap of the tent, and stepped outside. "Oh, and did she happen to mention that she was once nominated for a Nobel Prize?" she whispered as I zipped the flap closed.

11

"They Will Never Know"

We took off walking away from the lodge toward the back of the compound. It turned out there were eleven tents along our path, spread out with plenty of lawn between them so they felt really private. At first we were walking behind a couple, but they went into the fifth tent. We heard the sound of a man's voice and heard the woman laugh. Past their tent the path curved, and suddenly the only sound we could hear was the loud chirping of crickets and the *caw caw* of a bird somewhere up ahead.

Two tents had lights on—in one of them, someone coughed and broke the silence—but except for that, there weren't any human sounds. It was a lot darker here, too, so far away from the light coming from the lodge. I was glad Lucas had the flashlight.

We'd gone a long way without talking when suddenly Lucas stopped, grabbed my arm, and put her finger to her lips in a *Shh!* sign. A second later I heard what she'd heard: the sound of laughter. All-too-familiar laughter. Tinkly laughter.

"Her tent's there," Lucas whispered, pointing to the next one up. "I wonder who she's talking to."

Now Maria was saying something. We took a few more steps down the path, and although we still couldn't hear any actual words, the voice was clearer.

Lucas leaned over and breathed in my ear, "Let's get closer and hear what's going on. She might be talking to her accomplice!" Obviously, Lucas wasn't going to let go of her suspicion that Maria was in on the smuggling.

She put out her flashlight. I looked behind us. No one was coming.

We kept walking until we were past Maria's entrance path, then we moved onto the lawn and, step by silent step, crept closer to the side of her tent.

Before we were even near enough to hear the words, I'd figured out two things. First, Maria was talking on her phone, and second, she was talking to a guy.

There would be a gap of silence, then her little tinkle tinkle, and she'd say something in a flirty voice. It was like that over and over again.

We could see light from the mesh window that was open at the side, but the front of her tent was closed up, thank goodness, so she couldn't see us coming. We were almost right up to the corner of the tent when we heard her words for the first time.

Her laugh, then, "Reggie, I didn't say there was any-thing between us. Yet. I simply said that you now had a bit of competition to keep you on your toes."

I began to feel guilty. I saw the Ghost of Mom again. This time she was watching us, and in my picture, she was standing with her arms folded and an angry frown on her face. Mom definitely does not approve of listening to other people's private conversations.

But Mom wasn't there, and Lucas was my best friend, so instead of hurrying down the path, I put my mouth practically up against Lucas's ear and breathed, "We'd better get behind the tent so we can't be seen by anybody coming."

Lucas nodded, tiptoed up to the corner of the tent, and dropped to the ground because of the open mesh window. She started to crawl, the skirt she'd worn to din-ner hiked up around her waist so she wouldn't trip on it. I was on my hands and knees behind her, unfortunately forced to stare directly at her panties, holding the hem of my flared skirt between my teeth.

Lucas hadn't crawled for more than a few seconds when suddenly she gasped, rose up on her knees, and reared backward, actually hitting my head with her butt.

I was afraid Maria might have heard the gasp, but the sound must have been drowned out by another one of her laughs, because a few seconds later, she said, "I didn't know you were quite so devoted," in her flirty voice.

Lucas had become frozen in space, body pulled back,

shoulders hunched, arms clasped close to her chest, and head turned to the side, as if she was afraid of something right in front of her face.

I got on my knees behind her and peered over her shoulder. Caught in the light from the mesh window was a big, ugly spider, dangling from a strand of silk it had spun.

Great. A spider. The only thing in the world Lucas was afraid of.

I heard the sound of voices and looked back down the path. A couple was coming, walking hand in hand, close enough to be visible in the little lights along the walkway.

There wasn't enough room for both Lucas and me on the side of the tent between the corner and Maria's open window, and I was still visible. Any minute now the man and woman would get nearer, and when they did, they couldn't miss me.

I wanted to say, *Just crawl under the meeping bug!* But we were so close, I was afraid Maria would hear even the smallest whisper.

I took the edge of my skirt in my mouth again, dropped onto my belly, and scooted as quickly as I could around Lucas and beyond the spider, the bare skin of my legs sliding smoothly over the cool grass. Slowly, slowly, I rose just far enough to peek through the window at Maria. The head of her bed was up against the opposite canvas wall and she was lying there resting on a huge pile

of pillows that left her almost sitting up, but she was looking down at her fingernails, not at my face.

I reached up and broke the strand of spiderweb, and
when the bug hit the ground I squished it with my skirt
wrapped around my hand.

The next instant, Lucas was on her belly behind me,
and seconds later we were on our knees behind the solid
canvas at the back of the tent, only a couple of yards away
from a strip of trees and bushes.

The voices we'd heard were coming closer, speaking
in a foreign language. I wasn't sure, but I thought it was
Italian.

Where we were in the back, we were separated from
Maria by her bathroom. Her voice was muffled as it came
through one small window high up over our heads, but
we could still hear her. Now, instead of flirtatious, she
sounded sarcastic. "Well, Reggie, I'm delighted at your
response. Perhaps you will be on time on this occasion.
In contrast to your past behavior."

I peeked around the corner of canvas and saw the Italians (or whatever) on the sidewalk, still chattering away.

Maria had obviously heard them talking, too. Her
own voice dropped, and she continued, "Come in time so
we can at least have a drink here in the tent before we go
back out to your place. I have some good whiskey."

Now the Italians were unzipping the tent next door.

Another pause, and Maria laughed again, but this time

the tinkle wasn't as loud, and it sounded a little strained.

For the next minute or so the guy was doing the talking. All we heard from Maria was an occasional comment: "Yes, he is," "I'm not sure," and "Perhaps that's a good idea." During this whole time she didn't laugh once.

When she did laugh, she sounded nervous. "You wouldn't really do that just for me, would you?"

Finally, she said, "All right, tomorrow night at six thirty. You will be here on time, I take it."

Another pause.

"No, they will never know."

Lucas and I looked at each other. Who were *they*, and what would they never know?

Finally Lucas tapped her watch and mouthed, "We'd better go."

She pointed and gestured to a route behind the Italians' tent and stood up.

Suddenly a big dark shape flew out of the brush behind us. "*Caawww*," it screamed, and flapped its wings inches in front of Lucas's face.

Startled, she let out a little cry.

"Wait, someone's outside!" Maria's voice sounded alarmed.

I grabbed Lucas by the elbow and pulled her into the woods, where we crouched down behind a flowering bush. The sound of my pumping heart was loud in my ears.

"Who's there?" Maria called. She was out of the tent

now. Between the branches I saw the beam of her flashlight dart back and forth. Could she see the light color of our clothes and skin through the leaves and flowers? We huddled there not moving, not even daring to breathe in case we'd rustle the shrubbery. She would come after us, I just knew it.

It was probably fifteen seconds before I realized I still had hold of Lucas's elbow. I gave it a good squeeze and slowly, silently let out the breath I'd been holding.

At last we heard Maria zip her tent closed, then more zippers as she raised the flaps of her windows. When she spoke again, her voice was so muffled we couldn't hear her words.

I finally sucked in another breath, and for the first time I smelled the flowers surrounding us.

"I think the coast is clear," Lucas whispered.

We moved out from the bushes and quickly ran behind the tent next door and the dark tent after that, the very last one in that row.

"Holy schmack!" Lucas whispered when we were back on the path. "I'm sorry for making that sound. The spider was bad enough. But the bird startled the living meep out of me."

"Me too, even though it didn't come at my face."

A few steps later, at the very end of the path, instead of the brick fence that surrounded the rest of the compound there was a row of trees growing so close together they seemed to be tangled up in each other. In front of the trees was a high wire fence. One dim yard light next to the sign lit it up enough to read.

EUPHORBIA INGENS
CAUTION
Contact with this tree can burn the skin and cause blindness. The candelabra tree serves as a "living fence" to protect this compound from animals.

Every tree looked like a skinny version of those candelabras spooky people carry around in old monster movies. The kind with lots of candles. Bare branches came out of the trunk just above the ground. Instead of growing out horizontally, like on other trees, they curved at the ground like those candelabras, then grew straight upward, ending almost level across the top. There, at the very tip, leaves sprouted out, like flames on candles.

Off to one side, also lit by the yard light, was a bench. We'd spent a couple of minutes in our own tent, and the business with Maria had taken a good ten minutes, but we still had a few minutes to wait. It got darker as we sat there because suddenly every other one of the little white lights along the path went out. We didn't talk. It wasn't exactly quieter—the crickets had gotten even louder than they'd been before—but there were no more bird calls, no grunts from animals, no sounds from the bar, nothing but chirping.

Nothing.

Suddenly two figures stepped out of the darkness and a guy's voice said, "*Jambo.*"

12

Anya, Sam, and Waiting
for the Other Shoe

Sam and Anya walked into the dim circle of light. Lucas and I must have looked terrified, because Sam said, "I am sorry, we did not mean to startle you."

"Thank you for coming," Anya said. That sober, worried look she'd had at dinner was still on her face.

Sam gestured for Lucas and me to sit on the bench, then he and Anya dropped to their knees and sat on their heels facing us, moving slowly in a way that looked totally easy and natural, like ballet dancers might do it. I figured I'd have to practice months or maybe even years to do it that way.

Both Sam and Anya had changed out of their uniforms. They both wore dark pants and dark shirts. I wondered if they'd dressed that way so if they saw anybody from the lodge they could disappear into the darkness.

"Anya," I said, "what's wrong? You look like something's happened."

Sam turned toward Anya and took her hand. Obviously the two of them were boyfriend and girlfriend.

"Yes, something has happened." She was looking at us, holding her head up like the strong woman she wanted to be. "Perhaps I should not have asked you to come here, but you wanted to know when you could meet Sam, and getting together at this time of night was the only way I could think of for all of us to talk in private after—after what happened."

"What *did* happen?" I asked.

She took a big breath and closed her eyes for a second. "I found out while we were serving dinner that my uncle has been arrested. His name is Lali. He is married to my father's sister, Margaret. They live in Narok."

We both nodded, remembering Narok and what Bernard had said as we drove through it.

"The police say they found some artifacts in the shed behind my uncle's home," Anya continued. "The same kind of artifacts that were smuggled out of the country. And I think—well, Sam and I think—that my father will be next." She closed her eyes tight, trying, I thought, to be brave and hold the tears back. But tears squeezed through anyway, her face crumpled, and she started to cry.

Sam put his arm around her and scrambled in his pocket for a handkerchief.

"You think he will be arrested?" Lucas asked softly.

Sam was the one to answer. "Yes, that is what we think. Anya's uncle is—"

He broke off, as if not knowing what to say next.

Anya finished blowing her nose and said, "My uncle is not a very good man. He has been in prison twice for theft. Now the police have arrested him for stealing the artifacts. But the police came to search his home this afternoon, after the news broke. We think there is something odd going on, that someone is spreading rumors and wants to make it look like Lali is guilty of this crime. Even though he has stolen things in the past, everyone in my family believes he is innocent this time."

"At dinner someone said there was a rumor that Bernard and his brother-in-law are doing the smuggling together," Lucas said.

"That is what Maria believes." Anya's voice was bitter. "She is one of the people who is spreading the rumor."

"But the others at the table totally think your dad is innocent!" I said.

"He *is* innocent. My father is *not a thief*." Anya's voice had risen a little, as if she wanted to shout this from the rooftops. Sam put his finger in front of his lips.

She lowered her voice. "I know for certain he would not do this. Since we were very small he has told my brothers and me never to steal, because stealing is wrong. He would never, ever take anything that was not his. Yes, my uncle has been imprisoned as a thief. But my father does not approve of my uncle, and only speaks with him because he wants to be kind to my auntie. He would never work together with Uncle Lali to take what was not his."

"She is right," Sam said, nodding his head firmly. "Anyone who really knows Bernard knows he would not steal."

I absolutely believed them. "That's what we think, too," I said.

Lucas, who did, after all, want to be a lawyer someday, asked about the evidence. "What about the artifacts they found in the shed?"

Sam said, "We think those artifacts were planted. By the person who committed the crime, or by someone who was working with him or was paid to put them there."

"That's terrible for your aunt and her family! But what does this have to do with Bernard?" I asked.

Anya, close to tears again, pulled in an uneven breath. "He will be next. You will see."

Sam added, "We are, as the expression says, *waiting for the other shoe to drop.*"

Anya nodded. "That is right. We don't know when it will happen, but we know it *will* happen. Someone is trying to put the blame on my father and my uncle, and neither of them is guilty."

"Trying to frame them," I said under my breath. Amazing how those cop shows improved my crime vocabulary.

"I suppose that is how you would say it," she answered.

"But how can they frame your father?" Lucas asked. "Won't the police find out the truth?"

"Many Kenyan police officers are corrupt," Sam said quietly. "They can be bribed. This is widely known. It is part of what we live with."

"Sometimes American police can be bribed, too," I said.

"Even in the place where we live, which is known for *not* being corrupt," Lucas added.

She was right about scandals in the Minneapolis and Saint Paul police departments, unfortunately. And of course half of those cop shows I watched were about police taking bribes and doing favors for people they knew, which is what corruption is all about. But the bribery of our policemen was not widely known, and we didn't think of it as part of what we lived with.

"Auntie Margaret *knows* her husband," Anya said, continuing with her story. "She says that when he is involved with a crime, he acts a certain way. He swaggers around and pretends to be a big shot. But this time he has not done this. Even when he comes home from the bar at night, he does not brag about what a rich, important man he is going to be. Instead he complains that there are no jobs for him. She says if he were smuggling these valuable things, he would brag about it, at least when he has had some beers."

I wanted to ask what they lived on and why Lali had

drinking money if he didn't have a job, but after what Maria had said about unemployment at dinner, I figured I knew the answer: Bernard was helping support his sister and her family. I suppose he couldn't help it if his brother-in-law used some of the money to go to the bar. I thought of my own father who drank too much, and how tough it would be to get him to stop drinking.

"It must be really hard for your whole family," Lucas said. "Who do you suspect?"

Sam said, "Many of the people at the lodge believe that the thief must be someone who works at the Simba Hill site. But Anya and I and some of our friends think it may not be that at all. There are some people from a Maasai village near here who we have never trusted. We think they act in a bad way, but the things they do have not been against the law. At least, we did not know of anything criminal in what they did. Now that this has happened, we wonder if they had a part in it."

"But how can *we* help?" I asked.

Sam and Anya looked at each other, then back to us.

"We are hoping you can visit the village and see if you can find anything suspicious," Anya said.

Lucas turned and glanced at me. I knew she would be even more eager to help solve the mystery if it had something to do with the Maasai tribe.

13

Chicks on a Mission

Sam took his arm from around Anya's shoulder and grabbed her hand again. "The Maasai people have lived on this land for many thousands of years. Tens of thousands. Perhaps more."

"In their legend, their ancestors lived in the Garden of Eden," Anya added.

I thought about the prehistoric skeletons that had been found at Olduvai Gorge. It went through my mind to wonder if they were Maasai ancestors, and I thought what a perfect Garden of Eden this part of the world would make, with all the animals and the beautiful trees and plants and flowers.

"Professor Wanjohi had his students search for another entrance to the cave at the beginning when they came to work here, but they did not find one," Sam said, bringing me back to the crime.

"But we believe some of the Maasai may know of a different entrance into the Simba Hill cave," Anya said. "And we believe *they* may be the thieves."

Sam said, "I'm sure you saw that there are many Maasai villages in the area around the Masai Mara."

We nodded.

"There is one village near here where many tourists go to see their way of life," Anya said. "The head of the village is a man named Jamison. He grew up in that village, but he went away to Nairobi to get his education. They say that when he came back, he had changed."

Sam took up where she left off. "The Maasai people have always been herders and measured their wealth by how many cattle they own and how many children they have. But money is important to Jamison, and he has found many ways for the people in his village to earn it. He has even found ways for people in other neighboring villages to earn money. The Maasai now are very poor because the drought has meant that they cannot have as many cattle as they once did, so it is good they have a way to make extra income. But Jamison takes part of what everyone makes and keeps it for himself and his family. This is not the traditional Maasai way."

"Since we heard the news this morning, we have been talking about this. We are wondering if Jamison and his sons know of another entrance to the cave," Anya said, "and if they have taken rocks from it to sell to collectors.

We are thinking these things because we are friends with a young Maasai warrior named Koyati. He comes every morning to the breakfast buffet to pose for photographs."

"He is from a village very close to Jamison's village," Sam added. "Jamison was the one who spoke with the people here at the lodge to ask if Koyati could come and stand and let tourists take his picture. Koyati was given permission to stand for this purpose, as long as the lodge does not have to pay him. Now he comes every day, people give him money to have their picture taken with him, and when he leaves here he must walk back to Jamison's village and give Jamison half of everything he earns before he goes home to his family. It is not right."

"Why didn't Jamison have one of his own sons come and pose for the tips?" I asked.

Anya was the one to answer. "Many tourists visit his village, and his sons are needed to sell things in the gift shop. They also give demonstrations of jumping competitions, and people take their pictures and they earn even larger tips than Koyati's."

Lucas said, "I guess that makes sense."

"In a greedy kind of way," I added.

"Koyati says he and the people in his own village do not know anything about the other entrance to the Simba Hill cave," Anya continued. "I believe him when he says this. He says that he and his family and everyone he knows feel sorry for the people in Jamison's village because they all seem to be afraid of Jamison and his sons. They know some of the people there, and they do not believe that these people know anything about the smuggling. Koyati and his family and friends believe Jamison is corrupt, as so many bad men in Africa are."

"So you want us to visit this village, right?" Lucas asked.

The two of them nodded.

"But what should we do when we're there?" I asked.

"You could look around," Anya said. "Maybe you would see something or hear something that would help us find out what is really happening."

Sam added, "But only if it is convenient for you. We do not want to ask anything of you that would ruin your visit to Kenya."

"Seriously," Lucas said, "I've always wanted to visit a Maasai village while I'm here."

I nodded. "She even said so to Professor Wanjohi, so there wouldn't be anything suspicious about it."

"I am so glad!" Anya said. For the first time since the two of them had scared the living daylights out of us by appearing out of the darkness, she gave a big smile.

Lucas looked at Anya. "We wanted to help you and your dad from the minute we found out Maria and whoever else suspected Bernard."

"But we didn't—or at least I didn't—think we could help," I added, "because . . . because there were so many people who *could* be guilty. People here at this lodge and other lodges, people in villages—"

"You've given us a toehold in the rock," Lucas said.

The other two looked confused.

"A place to start," I translated.

"Anya's family and I will be very grateful for your help. Anya and I are engaged," Sam said with a proud smile. "Our parents have given their approval. In two years, when she is eighteen and I am twenty, we are going to be married. It is very important that we prove her father is innocent. He needs the money from his job, not just for his own wife and children, but for many other people in his family.

"Anya will be all right of course. She has me." He raised his head a little, as if he was proud he could take care of her.

Anya looked at him with a loving smile. "We have each other," she corrected quietly.

"Last year I was supporting many people in my own family with the money I earned here," Sam continued, "but six months ago my uncle, who had been out of work, got a job fixing cars. My uncle now can support his own family and others in our family, and both Anya and I are able to save some of our money for the time when we get married.

"We will use the money to go back to Nairobi where Anya will study either to be a chef or to run a hotel—"

"I am trying to decide," Anya broke in.

"And I will get the education I need to be a safari guide," Sam continued. "Anya's father is teaching me how to drive. Driving well is a very important part of being a good safari guide. And we are both studying French and German so we can speak with more tourists."

He was proud of all of these things, and you could tell that he really wanted the two of them to reach their goals.

"But if Anya's father does not have a job, she and I may have to use our money to support her family. This would be the end of my dream of making a better life for her and for me, and for our children."

I bit my lip and looked at Lucas, then turned back to Anya and Sam. "We'll try to get out to the Maasai village as soon as we can. Tomorrow maybe."

"It is not always possible to visit the village," Anya said. "Many tourists go there, and you must have reservations. Perhaps you can go tomorrow, or perhaps you will have to wait for another time."

"One last thing," I said. "Anya, are you going to tell your dad that we're doing this? Trying to find out who *really* committed the crime?"

Anya's face was suddenly sober, and she looked almost panicked. "Oh no! And you must promise not to tell him! He would never approve of this. Never!"

"So . . . if he finds out you've asked us to do this, will he be mad at you?" Lucas asked.

Sam looked at Anya and shook his head back and forth quickly, the way you do when you give up on something. "He knows how stubborn she is once she gets an idea in her head."

"He is proud that I am a strong woman!" Anya said.

We were crawling into bed when Lucas whispered, "It won't be just solving a mystery. It'll be helping prove Bernard is innocent."

I knew what she meant even though what she said was pretty random. "It's like a mission. We're Girls on a Mission."

"*Chicks* on a Mission."

"I like that," I said, pulling the covers up to my chin. "It has a ring to it."

14

Game Drive

"Good morning. It is six o'clock."

At first I couldn't think where I was or whose voice was waking me up. Then I remembered. I was in Africa, and this was what they had in the tent camp instead of alarm clocks: one of the people who worked around the lodge, going from one tent to another, telling guests when it was time for them to get up.

And they get up early at these places, I found out. No sleeping in. Everybody wants to get out as fast as possible to look at the animals on what they called *game drives*.

We did, too. Of course we had a full schedule for the day, with a visit to the dig site for sure and, if we were lucky, also to the Maasai village. Even if we did both things, we'd probably also be able to see some animals along the way.

"I feel really odd about this," I said to Lucas as I was getting dressed. "It's like I'm cut in half. Half of me is really excited to go on our first real day in the game park, and the other half is worried about Anya and her dad."

"I know what you mean," Lucas said. "The thing is, though, assuming we go to the dig site to see the almost-scene-of-the-crime, and if we get to go to the Maasai village, both those things will be helping Bernard."

"But what about the rest of the time? It's going to be hard for me to keep my mind off what we heard last night."

"I think the most we can do for Anya is to ask Bernard questions."

"But not too many questions," I said, pulling on my sandals. "We don't want him or anybody else to know that we're trying to solve the mystery. And if there are bad guys running around, we don't want them coming after us."

"We also don't want your uncle to find out what we're doing. How much do you want to bet he'd try to stop us?"

The Ghost of Mom appeared again, but I ignored her. "I think we just have to act as normal as possible and do regular things."

Lucas grabbed her camera, I put the strap of the binoculars around my neck, and we headed for the tent door.

Breakfast was served out on the patio next to the open-air bar. The view was gorgeous, looking down beyond the sloping hill, past the high brick wall, and out over the countryside. The breakfast itself was another huge buffet with so many choices it was hard to pick, including a whole table full of different kinds of fruit. As if that wasn't enough, there was a guy in a tall white chef's hat making fresh omelets and little flat pancakes called crepes.

Both Lucas and I decided to have the crepes. As we waited for them to be made, we watched Koyati—it had to be him—standing in the corner of the patio. He was wrapped in a red plaid cloth and carried a long stick, as if to protect us. Once in a while, one of the other guests at the lodge would stand beside him and have someone take a picture, then hand him a tip.

By the time we got back with our crepes, Uncle Geoff and the other archaeologists were all at the table looking glum.

"We're going to be taking off in a few minutes," Uncle Geoff said. "Last night, the police arrested Bernard's brother-in-law for the smuggling."

Somehow it hadn't occurred to me that anybody at breakfast would be talking about what we'd learned from Sam and Anya the night before. But I did my best to seem surprised.

"Oh, no!" I said, putting on my best act, and Lucas said, "That's terrible!"

Uncle Geoff nodded, agreeing. "The professor," he moved his head toward Professor Wanjohi, who looked our way, "is going into Narok to see if he can get him out on bail."

"The poor man is innocent!" the professor said. "I have no doubt he's been framed." His eyes flickered over to Maria, whose eyes quickly lowered to her bowl of granola and yogurt.

Lucas and I looked at each other. Maria had been right the night before when she said the professor wouldn't be pleased to hear her say she thought Bernard and his brother-in-law were responsible for the smuggling.

With all this going on, I thought maybe the professor wouldn't want us to come out to the cave that day. But when I asked if he wanted to postpone the visit, he flashed a smile. "Oh, you must come today! It will be a pleasure to show you around. I will probably be gone for a good share of the morning. Would you like to come for lunch? Bernard will have arranged some box lunches for you to eat while you're out on your game drive. You could eat them with us instead."

"That would be super," I said, "if you're sure."

"I'll mention it to Bernard on the way out."

Finally he and the others took off, leaving Lucas and me alone at the table.

The minute they were gone, I looked around to make sure nobody was listening and said, "Did you see the dirty look the professor gave Maria when he was talking about how Bernard's brother-in-law had to be innocent?"

"I wonder if he's asked himself if she could be in on it," Lucas said, reaching for her cup of hot chocolate.

Her enthusiasm for Maria as a suspect was beginning to get my own suspicions aroused. "In-ter-esting. Ver-y in-ter-esting."

I took my last bite of crepe and washed it down with what was left of my mango juice. "One thing I thought of was, now that we know, like, officially about Anya's uncle being arrested, we can ask Bernard about him."

Lucas nodded. "That's what I was thinking."

"It's bad news for Bernard and his family. We need to be sympathetic and not seem too excited about our day, even if we do get to see animals and go to the dig and maybe to the village and everything."

"Good point. It's an exciting day for us, but we don't want to seem like insensitive ghouls."

"Or insensitive goils," I said and raised my eyebrows.

Lucas groaned. "That's the worst joke I've heard in weeks. Maybe ever."

"Yeah," I said, with a grin. "I thought it was a pretty bad one, too."

Before we went back to our tent together, we stopped by Bernard's table and asked about going to the Maasai village that day or the next.

"I will call ahead and see when they will have time for you." His tone of voice didn't sound as enthusiastic as it had when he was talking the day before. I wondered if that had to do with the Maasai village or just with Lali being arrested.

✠   ✠   ✠

By seven thirty, the three of us were in the van, heading out. *Safari* meant journey, so yeah, we'd been on safari the day before. But this felt like the real thing, and it was exciting.

As we drove out of the gate, Bernard said, "The call to the Maasai village was successful, and after the Simba Hill dig, we will go directly there."

"Thank you for calling." Lucas was smiling, but it was obvious to me she was trying not to sound too excited or anything.

We started out talking to Bernard about meeting Anya by the pool, and how nice she was, and seeing her at dinner again. He beamed the whole time. He was obviously very proud of his daughter.

"Bernard, we heard that Anya and Sam are engaged," Lucas said. "Congratulations!"

Bernard nodded and said, "Yes, they expect to be married when they have saved enough money."

"They are quite young," I said.

Lucas turned as if to say something to me, but then seemed to stop herself and waited for Bernard to talk.

"In many places in Kenya and other African countries, people marry at younger ages than is common in the West."

"They're both such nice people," I said.

"Yes, they will make a fine young couple, I believe," he concluded.

I let a little while pass, then said, "Um, Bernard, we heard at breakfast about what happened to your brother-in-law."

"Yes, we are very sorry about that," Lucas added.

Bernard's eyes in the rearview mirror said that he was worried, but trying very hard not to *look* worried.

"Yes, it is very bad for my sister, Margaret. You probably also learned that Lali, her husband, has been arrested before. But I know in my heart he is not guilty of this crime. No matter what the police found."

"Do you have any idea who might be the real thief?" I asked.

"None. Some people talk about this person or that person, but it is all just gossip. I do not like to repeat gossip."

"Maria thinks your brother-in-law is guilty," Lucas said. No need to mention that she also thought that *Bernard* was guilty. "Besides Maria, who else thinks that?"

"Well, one is the man who pilots the balloon safaris over the Masai Mara." He pointed ahead of us. "One of his balloons is landing right now."

Sure enough, there up ahead, a colorful red and gold hot air balloon was coming gently down, down out of the sky.

"We're scheduled to go on the balloon safari day after tomorrow. I can hardly wait!" Lucas said in an excited voice.

If you had to pick a word to describe what I was feeling about the balloon safari, *excited* would definitely not be it. Lucas's parents had arranged for the two of us to take the morning balloon ride over the Masai Mara while we were here. It was, like, a big deal, and I got the impression it was pretty expensive. Mostly I'd spent a lot of time trying not to think about it.

The thing was, I really didn't want to go. I'm not just afraid of heights, I'm absolutely terrified of them, and the thought of getting so far up over the ground in nothing but a big wicker basket made me almost sick to my stomach.

I'd said this to Lucas a couple of times in the weeks before our trip, but I guess because she's so brave, she couldn't seem to understand that I was serious about it. But I *seriously* didn't know if I could get up enough courage to go. The things I'd read about balloon safaris made the ride itself sound really beautiful. There were tons of things to see. The trouble was that you were up in the air when you saw them.

The web page about the ride said that after the balloon landed—they always took off at dawn—the balloon company set up a big, long table and a portable stove right in the middle of whatever field they'd landed in, and all the passengers were served a super fancy breakfast. The trouble with *that* was, breakfast would probably not taste very good for me or for any of the other passengers if yours truly had spent the entire balloon ride throwing up out of panic.

I didn't say anything now, too embarrassed to let Bernard know how scared I was. Instead I just sat in my seat and repeated the same thing I'd been telling myself since the whole subject of the balloon came up: *You don't have to go, Kari. You don't have to go.*

I was glad when, a few minutes later, Bernard took my mind off the heights thing. "We are very lucky today," he said. "Look over there."

Off in the distance were two rhinos. The van came to a stop, its top opened up, and we stood to take a look. Lucas took a picture. I looked at the rhinos with my binoculars. It was amazing. I could see their eyes, could watch them take bites of the tall grass and chew. They were right there, half a football field away from me.

"Those are black rhino," Bernard said. "You must be very special people. We hardly ever see black rhino in the Masai Mara. Only a few of them are left here. Perhaps fewer than three dozen."

Lucas lowered her camera. "I've read how rare they are. We're *really* lucky!"

While Lucas and I were looking, Bernard was saying something—in Swahili, I figured, anyway I didn't understand it—into a two-way radio he had on his dashboard. He hung up at the same time we sat back down.

"I was calling my mates to tell them to come and look," he said. "The guides keep in touch to help each other make the best trip possible for our passengers. Now they will all come rushing here to look at the rare black rhino."

Sure enough, just then we saw a van and a Land Rover heading toward us from two different directions, plumes of dust behind them as they sped over the gravel roads.

"The first game drive, and the first of the Big Five that you see is the black rhino!" Bernard said as we started up again. "I do not think I have ever had this happen with my passengers before."

"Big Five?" I asked. "What does that mean?"

I saw Bernard look at Lucas in the rearview mirror. "Lucas, do you know?" he asked.

"I did know, but I think I've forgotten some of them," Lucas answered. This was astonishing, to have her actually forget something.

"How many do you remember?" Bernard asked.

"Let's see. Lion for sure."

He nodded.

"Elephant."

Another nod.

"Rhino."

"Not just any rhino. It must be a black rhino. Not everyone knows this, but it is true."

"Only black rhino? Really?" she asked.

Nod.

"Was another one the cheetah?"

Bernard shook his head. "Leopard. And the last one

is the cape buffalo. That list was made when there were hunting safaris. These were supposedly the most danger- ous animals. But it should really be the Big Six, because the hippopotamus is also very dangerous."

In the next hour we saw a hyena hiding in the bushes, and some hartebeest, and Grant's gazelles, two kinds of antelope that both had sets of horns so absolutely gor- geous I can't even describe them. When we saw a big group of impala, Bernard said, "Look at the McDonald's arches on their rumps." Sure enough, on each side of the tails of the impala there was a steep, black arch that stood out against their tan coats.

It was no trouble keeping my mind off the smuggling and the arrest and everything when we were looking at animals, because every time we saw a bunch of them my heart pounded with excitement. I couldn't even believe how amazing it was to be there, seeing them live and up close.

But during the beginning of our drive, every time we *weren't* looking at animals, I felt kind of guilty about not doing anything to help Anya and her father. We'd already asked Bernard all the questions I could think of without sounding obvious about trying to solve the mystery of the smuggling. Still, it felt like there was more I should be doing. I looked out the window, but I didn't really see anything. I was thinking about how the lives of Anya and Sam would change if Bernard went to jail.

We stopped to look at a kind of antelope called a topi, which was standing all alone in the middle of some trees. Bernard raised the top of the van and Lucas took a picture. When we were on our way again, I suddenly realized that I could hardly remember anything about the animal I'd just seen because I'd been busy the whole time thinking about Bernard and his brother-in-law and Sam and Anya and the missing artifacts.

The Ghost of Mom appeared again, and for a change, she wasn't ticked off at me, just giving me advice. Typical. In my mind I heard her saying, "Stay in your day, Kari."

What she means when she says that is that you could pretty much ruin your life by spending all your time thinking about what's already happened or worrying about what might happen, instead of concentrating on what's happening right now.

So I told myself we'd do our best to help Anya and her dad. In the meantime, I was going to stay in my day and not let what had happened the night before or what might happen in the future totally wreck our trip.

At that second we came around a bend, and it was almost like I'd been given a sign that I'd made the right decision. Off to the right were three elephants walking slowly, a big one with tusks in front, a smaller adult at the rear, and between them a little elephant, a third the size of the biggest one. They were so close I could see the individual wrinkles in their skin.

"What do you think of that?" Bernard said, raising the top of the van. "Have you ever heard of the song 'Baby Elephant Walk'?"

The name rang a bell, and suddenly the tune came to me and I started to hum it. Anya and Bernard and Lali and Sam were out of my head. I was right there in the van, looking at these awesome animals.

"Hey, we've already seen two of the big five!" I turned to Lucas. "Take a lot of pictures. I love elephants! It will be cool to have a picture of an elephant family!"

Lucas took her first shot and said, "It's probably more likely to be two female elephants. The females raise the calves together. The males usually spend their time with other males."

Lucas's facts were part of my day, too. But now that she wasn't giving me mini-lectures every five minutes, I could almost enjoy them.

15

Simba Hill

It was getting close to lunchtime, and Bernard announced we were heading for the Simba Hill dig. I tightened my fists and bit my lip in excitement. As I thought of this site and the way the archaeologists had described it, I suddenly came up with another question I could ask that maybe had something to do with the smuggling.

"Bernard, somebody told us that you had been a part-time guard at the Simba Hill site before we came. I was wondering about the other guard, the one that works full time. Prosper. Prosper is an interesting name."

"Prosper is not an unusual name, especially in the part of Africa south of here."

"What's he like?"

"I do not know Prosper very well." That's all Bernard said with words, but he stopped looking back at us in the rearview mirror, and his eyes said that whatever he knew about Prosper was something he didn't like.

❊   ❊   ❊

About a half hour later, we came to the turnoff to Simba Hill, and we started down a narrow track where wheels had worn into the grass.

The minute we turned, Bernard pulled a cell phone out of his pocket. "I will call to let them know we are getting close."

He talked for a minute as we bumped along. When he hung up, he said, "As I mentioned before, there is no mobile phone reception inside the cave, but I have notified Prosper, and he will tell the archaeologists. We'll be there in five minutes."

"Sweet!" I said, but it came out, "Swe-eet" because just as I said it we went over a bump in the road.

The bouncing didn't seem to bother Bernard. "Simba Hill is a *kopje*," he said. "Do you know what a *kopje* is, Lucas?"

"They're those big rock formations that stick out on the tops of hills." She turned to me. "Like Pride Rock in *The Lion King*. But in real life they're not as big as Pride Rock."

She looked at Bernard in the rearview mirror. "I thought they were mostly south of here, in Tanzania and maybe South Africa."

"You are correct again. There are not many *kopjes* in this area. The one here probably began at some point being just one large outcropping, but now it has split into smaller formations."

"How far are we from Tanzania?" Lucas asked.

"Not far. From here it is probably less than forty miles."

"Can we go there?" she asked.

"We cannot cross the border without visas. Why do you want to go to Tanzania?"

"I want to see my cow." She told Bernard about buying a cow for a Tanzanian family.

"I have an idea," I said. "Maybe we could get close to the border, and if the wind is in the right direction, we might be able to *smell* your cow."

"Very funny, Sundgren," Lucas said.

The track we were following took us into a grove of acacia trees with yellow bark and right down through a little stream and up the other side. We'd been bumping along for what seemed a long time when Bernard said, "Do not be surprised when you see Prosper standing with a gun at the Simba Hill site. Remember, he is the guard."

"You were the guard sometimes before Lucas and I got here. Do you still carry a gun?" Lucas asked.

"Yes, I am licensed to carry a gun. I keep it under the front seat."

At last, on top of an especially big rise covered with lots of trees and bushes, we saw a Land Rover. Beside it stood Uncle Geoff, Charlie, and Prosper in front of two giant reddish rocks that were at least twice as tall as Charlie.

As soon as they saw the van coming up the steep track, all three guys waved.

Bernard pulled up, and Uncle Geoff slid open the passenger door.

"*Jambo*," he said with a smile. "Welcome to Simba Hill!"

When we'd all jumped out, he turned and said, "Prosper, I'd like you to meet my niece, Kari, and her friend Lucas."

Close up, I noticed Prosper had a square face with what Mom sometimes calls *heavy features*: a biggish nose, big bones where his eyebrows were, and a wide mouth.

Bernard looked from Charlie to Uncle Geoff. "How did it go for the professor at the police station?"

They both shook their heads, looking grim, and Charlie said, "No luck. At least not this time. He says he's going to keep trying."

Bernard looked disappointed, and I didn't blame him.

The guys had been standing in front of a bunch of bushes completely covered with thorns almost as long as needles, with the enormous bare rocks behind. There wasn't an entrance to a cave, only a path through the bushes leading into a crevice between the two rocks.

"Wow. The cave is really well hidden!" Lucas said.

"It's even more hidden than it looks from here," Uncle Geoff said, gesturing toward a path that had steep walls of rock on both sides.

I could see what Bernard had meant about a big rock outcropping that had been split in different places.

"Girls, before we head onto the path, you'd better grab your sweaters," Uncle Geoff said.

We fished them out of our bags.

"I can take them back if you'd like to stay here," Bernard said to Prosper.

Prosper turned one of his palms up, as if it didn't matter to him one way or the other. So while Bernard grabbed his gun, we got in line behind Charlie, with Bernard bringing up the rear.

Charlie led us between those first rock walls, then zigzagged through formations that stood so close together there was room for only a narrow path and, here and there, some bushes.

"Look out for the thorns," Charlie said as he moved carefully to avoid a branch. "I understand they hurt like the very devil."

I glanced back, and there was Bernard, right behind Uncle Geoff. When he saw me looking, he said, "There are many wild animals in the park, so I am here to protect you. Perhaps there are lions watching us right now."

Of course I knew from *The Lion King* that *Simba* meant *lion*. But cartoon characters were one thing, and real lions were another. The thought of them made me shiver.

We hadn't gone much farther when Charlie stopped suddenly and his arm shot into the air, the hand open to tell everybody behind him to be still.

We stopped walking, stopped talking. I stopped breathing. Bernard darted toward Charlie, moving around us on our right, gun raised, his feet making no sound at all.

In the sudden silence, I heard a rustling up ahead in the bushes beside where Bernard now stood, looking down the length of his gun.

I expected either a shot or that some animal would come charging at us out of the brush. What came instead was a scream. *"Aieeeeeee!"*

It was Bernard, yelling at the top of his lungs. The sound scared the meep out of me. It must have scared whatever was in the bushes, too, because the next thing we heard was another rustle, which died away.

Bernard lowered the gun. "It is gone now. We can go on."

I let out a huge breath of relief.

"What *was* that animal?!" Lucas asked.

He shrugged. "I am not sure. I know by the sound it made that it was too large to be a dik-dik and too small to be a full-grown lion, so it could be many things. Because this is a hill where there are many lions, most other animals that are their prey stay away from it. I am guessing it was a lion that is not yet fully grown, or possibly a hyena. They come from time to time to see if the lions have left any carcasses they can clean up."

"Do people from here always yell like that to chase animals away?" I asked. My voice trembled a little.

"It is one thing we try. Sometimes it frightens them, sometimes it doesn't. When you are often around danger-ous animals, you learn what to do at different times to keep the animals away from you." He made it sound like less of a big deal than *I* thought it was.

Uncle Geoff looked at Bernard, and said, "Thank you very much. Personally, I'm not *quite* ready to become part of the circle of life."

16

Tension in the Cave

At last the path twisted around, and suddenly we were looking at what seemed to be a mud hut sticking out of the huge rocky cliff behind it. Next to the steel door on the front were shovels and picks and things that looked like tool kits, brooms, buckets, and an enormous piece of noisy machinery chugging away.

"That's an electricity generator so we can have electric lights and use our computers and printers and things in the cave," Charlie said. "Runs on diesel. Smells lovely, doesn't it?"

I wrinkled my nose. "Yech. Diesel fuel. It's gross."

He opened the door. "Welcome to our humble site," he said, and stood aside for the rest of us to go in.

Bernard stayed outside, and Lucas, Uncle Geoff, and I stepped over the electric cables into the tiny entryway, then into the cave itself.

The room was as big as a medium-sized house. It had dirt floors full of big square or rectangular holes, and rock walls. Floodlights lit up tables set near the walls. The smell was a combination of dirt and diesel. But what I mostly noticed was that Professor Wanjohi and Maria were at the back of the room, and although they were quiet now, it was obvious they'd been arguing. You could practically feel the anger in the air.

Uncle Geoff, maybe sensing the same thing I did, said, "Time to put on your sweaters, girls. It's as cold as a refrigerator in here."

He picked his own sweater up from a nearby table and pulled it on, and Charlie got into his fleece.

While I unwrapped my sweater from where the sleeves were tied around my waist, I heard Lucas breathe in my ear, "What the meep is up here?"

I looked out of the corner of my eye at Maria. Although her mouth was smiling for us, her eyes weren't smiling at all. She kept glancing over at Professor Wanjohi with an expression that looked ticked off.

The professor ignored her and walked toward us on planks that ran alongside a deep trench leading down the center of the cave room. He had a real smile on his face.

"Welcome! So good to have you here!" he said.

As he came toward us, I felt his energy again. I remember hearing about somebody—maybe it was a movie star or a president—who "filled up the room." It seemed like the professor filled up that whole big space. In a good way.

Rather than following him, Maria came a different route, zigzagging to avoid the huge holes in the cave floor, all of which had planks lying along each of their four sides. Some also had plank walkways across them.

The professor looked at Lucas and me. "We've been very busy in here, as you can see." He looked down to let us know he was talking about the holes in the floor. "This was all accomplished thanks to student labor," the professor said. His eyes twinkled. "Or, as the students prefer to think of it, deliberate torture."

"I was being tortured right alongside them," Charlie said. "Every muscle in my body hurt for months." He gave me a stern look, his forehead wrinkled in a frown. "Think carefully before you choose archaeology as a profession, young lady."

I smiled, and Uncle Geoff turned to me. "Remember how I told you about the symmetrical holes archaeologists dig? Well, this is what they look like. These are based on cubic meters, which are quite common."

"Why not just dig up the whole thing?" Lucas asked.

I knew why not, but I thought it might be showing off to answer.

Uncle Geoff looked at the professor, who said, "Archaeology is a destructive science, Lucas. By digging, we are disturbing artifacts and taking them from their prehistoric home. We are taking samples only. The rest remains in place. We want to preserve history, not destroy it."

"You dug all of this using trowels?" I asked.

Charlie nodded. "We dug it with what is essentially a common garden trowel. Every bloody square inch. And sifted every microscopic grain of dirt through screens." He closed his eyes and shuddered.

Maria, who had been standing away from the others with her arms folded, came forward. "You'd never know it from the way he complains, but Charlie is a fine and dedicated archaeologist." She turned toward Uncle Geoff with a smile. "Your uncle taught him well."

"Aww, Charlie, you're blushing! How sweet!" Uncle Geoff said, trying to ignore Maria's come-on, I thought. But Charlie's cheeks actually were turning pink.

Maybe to rescue Uncle Geoff, or maybe just to change the subject back to how archaeologists work, Lucas asked, "How careful do you think the smugglers were about getting the treasure out? Would they have had to use trowels and screens to dig up the things they smuggled without ruining them?"

"That's a very good question, Lucas," the professor answered. "It's something the people at the British Museum will be looking into. Charlie, Geoff, and I were talking about that very subject in the airplane on the way out from Nairobi."

He looked at Uncle Geoff, who said, "They could have gone about it one of two ways. If they were very rough in their methods, they could have destroyed many pieces, but managed, by luck or some care, to salvage a few.

"Of course, we're hoping they worked more carefully—although probably not as carefully as we would—and managed to preserve much of what they found. In which case, the site, wherever it is, could be in relatively good shape for future archaeological study.

"But they may have taken much of the art available there. If they've been careful, and they worked over a long period of time, they may have unearthed many specimens. Some may have gone out of the country already. Some may still be somewhere around here, hidden in a safe place."

"Let's say they were more careful," Lucas said. "Would that mean they'd have to be, like, archaeologists themselves?"

Uncle Geoff shook his head. "Archaeological methods are no secret, really. Anyone who wanted to find out how we work could get all the information they needed in a couple hours on the Internet."

Lucas sighed. I figured she'd been hoping to get evidence she could use to pin the blame on Maria.

"We've talked about techniques long enough," the professor said. "Come over and see what we've discovered. Of course we've unearthed a variety of things, tools and so on, and some bones. But it's the art you must see. It's quite extraordinary."

He led us between the holes in the ground and across a wooden walkway to one of many long tables that sat along the sides of the room. They were set up so they didn't block the entrances to the two passages leading out of the big room into other parts of the cave. As we followed the professor, I noticed that one of the tables was stacked with all kinds of brushes and jars and trowels and things. Two had laptops on them, and others were covered with white sheets.

Professor Wanjohi went to one of the covered tables and pulled the sheet back. "Aren't they beautiful?"

Lined up in three neat rows on the table were about twenty rocks of different sizes, from round ones as small as apricots to one flat one as big as a dinner plate. Some had pictures scratched into the surface. I knew the scratched ones were called petroglyphs. The ones that were painted—some in red, some in black—were pictographs. Each rock was in a clear plastic bag that also held a label.

I gasped, and Lucas said "Awesome!" I knew that mostly she was interested in how what she saw in the cave related to the crime, and she didn't care about archaeology the way I did. But she's an artist herself, and you could tell by her voice and the look on her face that when she saw the art, she really loved it.

Uncle Geoff smiled at our reaction and reached under his sweater to get his glasses from his shirt pocket.

Every picture was of either an animal or a human. They didn't have a lot of details, but you could see what each of them was. A giraffe, a rhino, an elephant, and two that I thought were probably wildebeest, which I'd seen on nature programs. Five of the figures were long, graceful human shapes.

My favorite was a pictograph of an impala with those horns curving back. I was looking at it, wishing I could touch it, when Professor Wanjohi carefully took it out of the bag and said, "You mustn't touch the drawing part, but you can touch the side of the rock if you want to, Kari."

I reached up to the stone and let my finger stay there for a second before I moved on.

"You too, Lucas," the professor said, and Lucas smiled at him before she put her finger on the rock.

I'd sort of forgotten about Maria for a minute there, but now she said, "Note that the specimens on this table include some that were once on the walls, and some that never were."

Uncle Geoff glanced over at me, his eyebrows raised. "And what do you call the different kinds?"

I rolled my eyes, embarrassed, and said, "The ones that are on a wall are parietal. Mobiliary means you can carry them around."

"I'm very impressed!" the professor said.

Uncle Geoff grinned at me. "You get an A plus on that pop quiz, kiddo."

Professor Wanjohi moved to another table. "Now look at this," he said, pulling back the sheet.

Right in the middle was a big engraving that had been pieced together from five separate sections. There was a human figure with a stick in his hand facing a rhinoceros. Over to one side was a lion.

Now it was Maria's turn to do the explaining. "This is a fascinating piece from an anthropological perspective," she said. "Obviously, the human figure is a hunter stalking the rhino. What we've discovered by analyzing the individual strokes of the engraving is that the lion was added later, maybe as some sort of religious ritual. We know that engravings and other rock art were often done to add spiritual power to hunting expeditions before they set out."

I stared at the engraving and wondered about the people who drew pictures to give themselves power when they hunted. How did that work? Did they pray while they were doing it? Or did they think that just by creating a picture of the lion, they'd get the lion's strength?

Lucas was looking from the large engraving to the stones on the other table. "These don't all look alike," she said. "I mean, they look like they were done by different artists."

Again, Maria was the one to answer. "From some of the evidence we've found, we believe an extended family may have lived in this space for many years, and drawing may have been a skill and tradition passed along from generation to generation."

"There are some remaining parietal specimens in the two passages," the professor said, pointing at the openings that led from this room farther into the hill. "You can see them after lunch."

That seemed to remind him, because he said, "But how thoughtless of me! You're probably hungry. We have lunches here, so let's partake."

"No chairs, so pull up a plank," Charlie added. He pointed to a place toward the end of the long, central trench where boards had been set along both edges and across the excavated trough itself, making a rectangle where people could sit and look at each other while they ate, their legs dangling. "It's humble, but we like to think of it as home."

"Careful that you don't kick the sides and disturb the soil," Uncle Geoff said.

As I took a box lunch and a bottle of soda out of a cooler on the floor, I thought about the artifacts we'd just been looking at. About the person who'd drawn that beautiful picture of the impala, and how smooth and cool the stone had felt under my finger. It was something somebody had picked up and worked on thousands of years ago, and I had touched it. Whoever had painted it had been dead for all those years. But what they'd drawn was still there, and would probably be there for thousands of years more. That's something I always think about when I see really ancient art: people don't last, but the things they make sometimes do. It's what makes me want to be an archaeologist. When it's art like that picture of the antelope, anyone who saw it any time in those thousands of years would think it was beautiful. It's like a little part of the artist lives forever.

Everybody settled down and dug into the food. It was quiet for a minute, then Lucas, in her Lucas-like, totally un-shy way, said, "So, what do you all think about the smuggling?"

17

Maria Suffers, Poor Dear, and Artifacts and Reverence

"We've been doing a lot of thinking about that." Professor Wanjohi swept his short, broad hand around in his energetic way to show that he was talking about himself, Maria, and Charlie.

"The one thing we're sure of—and perhaps the only thing we're sure of—is that none of the pieces we've catalogued so far has gone missing. They're all still in this room. The people at the British Museum sent their analysis and images of some of the rocks that were looted, and we're sending our own analyst to London with samples from the dig for a side-by-side comparison. But given what we've seen, we strongly believe that the rocks came from the Simba Hill cave.

"As I mentioned when we were in Nairobi, there may be another entrance. In fact, there may be several. We had our student team conduct a search for another way into the cave when we first arrived here, and they found nothing." He used another sweeping gesture, this time with both his arms, to show the searching was done in a big area.

"Do you have any idea who took the rocks that were in that suitcase?" Lucas asked.

"None." The professor said this loudly and with a firm shake of his head. His eyes flicked over to Maria. She quickly looked down at the floor and folded her arms in front of her.

"How about the students who were here?" Lucas asked.

The professor said the students had all gone home more than two weeks before. As for stealing the artifacts, it was almost impossible that they'd been involved. When they were at the site they were always working with other people.

"About the only time they were by themselves was when they went to the portable toilet that's behind one of the rocks outside the entrance," Maria said. "We all agree there's no practical way any of the students could have been involved in this."

She turned quickly to Professor Wanjohi, then back to us. Something was going on, and I would have bet a thousand bucks it had to do with Maria thinking Bernard was guilty.

Charlie tried to cover the next awkward moment,

saying, "When we're finished here, I'll show you some of the things I've been washing in those two big tubs over there." He gestured with his head. "You can't really see them from here, but there are some nice pieces. Tools and pots, mostly, and some of the rock art that I've brushed and cleaned without water because they can't be washed for one reason or another. Then you'll have to go back to where Maria and Geoff are working on some 3-D images, and take a look at what the professor is doing." With that, Charlie took a big bite of his sandwich.

"Why do you do all these things?" I asked.

Uncle Geoff put up his hand, as if to keep the others from answering. "This all has to do with context. How about I give a version of my Archaeology 101 introductory lecture about the importance of keeping artifacts in place?"

"Perfect," Charlie said. "I remember it well. My first day in class."

"Second day, actually," Uncle Geoff said. "My, how quickly my students forget." He sighed and rolled his eyes.

"Okay," he started, "as I tell my students, context is enormously important in evaluating artifacts. That's part of the reason we as archaeologists feel so strongly about the theft of artifacts from the sites where they were found. For example, at the Simba Hill site, take that big picture you saw on the table, the one with the hunter and the rhino and the lion. If somebody had roughly dug the pieces up and sold the engraved piece with the rhinoceros on it to somebody in New York, and the human figure to somebody in London, and the lion head to somebody in Hong Kong, the engraving itself, the artwork of it, would be all that any of the buyers could see. Even if they were displayed in museums. The pictures would have no story and no relationship to each other.

"Here at the dig, those pieces were excavated with care and reconstructed, and they've been analyzed stroke by stroke. That's how we've been able to figure out the meaning of the picture that Maria told you about. If they'd been dug out roughly and sold to various buyers, we wouldn't have been able to understand any of that."

I'd heard lectures like that from Uncle Geoff before so I didn't say anything, but Lucas nodded and said, "It helps me understand why you care about this—these old things."

When it was time for everybody to get back to work, Charlie showed us what he'd been washing and cleaning, then headed for the passage where Uncle Geoff and Maria had gone after lunch. "Okay, you guys—" he began.

Lucas interrupted. "We decided we're chicks."

Charlie nodded. "I stand corrected. Okay, you two *chicks*, you saw Maria and Geoff put on their hard hats before they went in?"

We nodded.

"You're next. Everybody has to wear a hard hat to go back into the passages." He grabbed three hard hats from a row next to passage entrance, kept one for himself, and gave the other two to us.

I fastened the strap. "I've never worn a hard hat before."

"They make you instantly important," Charlie said. He fastened his own strap and led us into the passage. Because he was so tall, he had to duck way over to get through the entrance. On the other side, he patted the top of his hard hat as if checking to make sure his head had made it through safely.

The minute we got inside the passage, we heard Maria's tinkling laughter.

Charlie looked over his shoulder at us and raised his eyebrows.

Up ahead, about halfway to where the passage completely collapsed, Maria sat on a chair with a computer in her lap, a hard hat covering her hair. Uncle Geoff wasn't visible.

"Come in and have a look at what Geoff and I are doing. It's fascinating work." She said it like she really meant it, and it struck me that behind all the bragging and ego stuff, Maria was not just a real archaeologist, but one who really cared about her work. The thought made me like her a little better.

When we got back to where her chair was set up, we

could see another passage that had led off it. The walls of that part had collapsed, too, leaving a small triangular space. Uncle Geoff was in there with a tripod and a camera. He smiled and greeted us, then swung the camera around so we could see that it had two side-by-side lenses.

"There's some art on the walls in here, but it's too narrow for a panoramic angle, so I'm taking lots of close-ups," he said. "Maria is working with them."

Lucas and I watched her use the mouse to pull the small images to where they belonged in a larger picture of a wildebeest, like pieces of a jigsaw puzzle. But the screen didn't show just the image on the wall, it also showed the roughness of the wall itself. It was like looking at a 3-D movie, only we didn't need special glasses.

"Wow!" I said.

"How cool is that!" Lucas sounded truly excited, even though this probably didn't have anything to do with the smuggling.

"It's wonderful to be working together with a consummate professional like Geoff," she said, and I swear she fluttered her eyelashes at him.

It was then that I came up with what I have to admit, thinking back, was one of my more brilliant ideas ever.

I turned to Uncle Geoff. Trying to make my voice sound all innocent, I asked, "Is this an image you could e-mail to Britt to show her what you've been working on?"

I heard air coming out of Lucas's nostrils as she tried not to laugh. At the same time, Maria's head snapped up and her shoulders suddenly looked tense. I would have given anything to see her expression.

Uncle Geoff slowly raised his head from the camera and looked at me without even the smallest trace of a smile on his face. "That's a great idea."

"Is she another archaeologist?" Maria asked in the sweetest possible voice.

"No, actually," Uncle Geoff said. "She's a weaver. She was going to come on this trip with me, but she'd already promised her family that she'd visit them over the holidays. She's from Norway."

I was pretty sure that the part about Britt almost coming on the Africa trip with him wasn't really true, but I understood why he said it.

"A Norwegian weaver. How . . . interesting." I wouldn't have been surprised if, instead, she'd said, *How nice for you.*

Uncle Geoff said he was at a good stopping point, and he followed us out of the passage.

Back in the big room, the professor was working on a 3-D image of two rhinos fighting, painted in black, getting the clearest possible look at every line in the drawing.

"What I'm doing is enhancing the images so that I can make a precise examination of each stroke. One of the things I've found out about *this* image is that the rounding of the belly was made with one single stroke. It's brilliantly executed."

His voice was kind of hushed when he said it. This was exactly how Uncle Geoff talked about artifacts they found on his archaeological digs. Mom had said once that he felt reverence about the artifacts he worked with, and I thought that was the right word for how the professor sounded now.

Uncle Geoff led us into the other branch of the cave where we saw some figures painted on the walls. My favorite was a very simple drawing of a man with a spear, leaping. It was absolutely gorgeous.

"So, what did you two think about what you saw today?" the professor asked. Everyone had come into the main room to say good-bye to us.

"It was wonderful!" I answered.

"Still want to be an archaeologist?" Charlie asked, looking at me over his glasses.

"More than ever!" I said, and I meant it. "And I totally get why you're so bummed by the looting."

"Who knows what they destroyed digging out the artifacts they found?" The professor closed his laptop, almost with a bang. "The people at the British Museum said some of the pieces had been shattered on the way."

Maria had seemed pretty sulky ever since she came back into the main room—poor dear, her dream of romance was as shattered as the rock art—but now her expression turned really angry. "They said one of the damaged pieces was an especially beautiful depiction of a man carrying a spear, very much like the parietal figure you saw in the passage. They fit it back together, but it's not the same."

I looked around at the sad and angry faces.

I knew one thing about the missing artifacts. No matter what Lucas thought about Maria being involved, she wasn't one of the looters. None of them was.

18

Odd Things at a Maasai Village

"There are a few things I should tell you about this village you will visit," Bernard said. It was more than an hour later, we were getting close to the village, and Lucas was getting more and more excited.

"Most Maasai people do not welcome visitors to their villages, and many do not like to have their pictures taken. But in this village, visitors are welcome, and anyone is allowed to take pictures. Of course, you are expected to leave a tip if you use your camera."

Tips had become no big deal. We were getting used to leaving them. Ever since our plane had landed we'd been giving dollar bills as tips to anyone who did even the smallest thing for us.

"All tips should be left with Jamison, the man who is the head of the village."

Lucas and I looked at each other. Sam hadn't mentioned that all the tips went directly to Jamison. I wondered if he knew.

"And they have a gift shop where you can buy things made by Maasai people from many miles around. The Maasai traditionally have made their living raising livestock. But the drought we have had here in Kenya for many years has made it more and more difficult for the animals to find food, so the people have had to make crafts and sell them. But I should warn you: much of what is displayed at the gift shop has not been made by the Maasai people at all, so be careful what you buy. Some of it is high quality, some of it is very badly made."

"Even if that's true, if the people around here are so poor, it still seems good that this village is willing to welcome tourists and have a gift shop, if they sell at least some things that are made by the Maasai," Lucas said. Obviously she was wondering what Bernard would say to this.

"Oh, the village does all right. They take a cut of everything they sell," Bernard said. I wasn't sure, but I thought maybe his voice sounded a little sarcastic. I noticed that he never really said anything bad about anybody. I admired him for not gossiping, even if I wanted to know more than he was telling us.

"Was it Jamison's idea to have the tourists visit this village?" Lucas asked. Again her voice sounded completely innocent, as if she didn't know the things Sam had told us about Jamison.

"Yes, he is very good at making money for his village."

"Are they getting rich, then?" I asked.

Bernard didn't answer right away. Finally he said, "I do not know what happens to the money."

He changed the subject. "Lucas, you are very interested in the tribes. What do you know about the Maasai culture?" Lucas was obviously thrilled he had asked her this question, because she started talking really fast again, like she had when she'd talked about the Rift Valley. "Well, first, they're a little like the Native Americans back where we come from, because they hold onto their culture even though it's very different from the rest of the world.

"One of the most important things for the Maasai people is the 'coming of age.' This is when a boy turns from an adolescent into a warrior, which they call *il Moran* in their language. The guys—the *Morani*—have to go through things that are really painful, but they can't show any pain. They get all dressed up, and wear jewelry, and do fancy things to their hair."

"The guys do?" I asked.

Lucas nodded. "When it was still legal to kill wild animals in Kenya, they had to kill a lion before they were considered men. Now they can only kill animals in self-defense, but that still includes killing lions when they have to. Many times they take the heads of the lions they have killed and preserve them for the guys to wear in ceremonies."

We were pulling up to the village now, close enough that I could see the thorns on the acacia branches that made up the wall.

"How much do you know about their sanitation?" Bernard asked.

"One website I was looking at said they use urine as a disinfectant."

"Not seriously!" I gasped.

Bernard pulled the van into the parking lot. "Lucas is correct. You may be shocked by the Maasai sanitation levels. Many Western visitors are quite disgusted. But you must realize that this aspect of their lives is to be respected as part of their tradition. Urine is actually sterile, so it is effective as a disinfectant. And the Maasai have very high rates of resistance to diseases that would easily kill everyone in this van if we lived the way they do."

Lucas was talking as we got out of the van, but this time I tuned her out completely. A tall man dressed in red cloth had opened the gate, and I was so totally overwhelmed by what I saw behind him that my mouth actually dropped open.

"Welcome to our village," the man said. His hair was going gray, but he was still handsome, and he had a good-looking smile. "My name is Jamison, and I will be your guide."

I just had time to think that Jamison didn't look like a bad guy before he turned and led us into one of the most amazing scenes I'd ever laid eyes on.

We were completely surrounded by mud huts shaped like large loaves of bread, with roofs made out of branches. The huts were all built close to the fence. The middle space looked and smelled like a barnyard, covered with fresh and not so fresh manure. About a dozen guys who were just a little older than we were, maybe sixteen or seventeen, were walking across the barnyard toward us, all of them with posture that was straight and tall and proud.

They were dressed the same, everybody wearing what looked kind of like loose, short sundresses made out of plain red cloth, fastened around the waist by a black rope or strap, with a spear dangling from the side. All but two of them wore jewelry around their neck and had long, long hair dyed a reddish color, and the most complicated hairdos I've ever seen, including on women. Every hairdo was different, and most of the guys had jewelry on their head or in their hair as well. There were cornrows and long braids with metal strands braided in, buns with jewelry in them at the back of the head, and headbands with silver discs dangling from little metal chains.

The young men lined up in front of us. And suddenly I understood why the guys did the hairdo and jewelry thing when they were looking for a wife. These guys were hot. Very, very hot. I think part of the reason was that at least in their culture, they looked good, and they held themselves tall and straight and proud partly because they knew it. If the warriors—what had Lucas called them, the

Morani?—wanted to get married, they probably had girls coming out of the woodwork.

Behind the guys were groups of girls and women, all of them with hair cut close to their heads. All were dressed in bright colors—yellow, turquoise, pink, lavender. There were children, too, some of them sitting near what looked like fresh manure.

Like I said, the place was absolutely amazing. I wondered if it bothered the people to be looked at this way, wondered if they liked Jamison's idea or if they hated having tourists come in and take their pictures. It made me feel a little odd about being there.

While I was thinking all of this, Jamison told us things about their village. He had a soft voice, which was surprising for a tour guide, and that good-looking smile was as white as Bernard's, although it probably wasn't quite as sincere. Of course, why should it be? He had to greet new groups of tourists hour after hour every day.

But he was handsome, no question about it. I thought that when he was young, he'd probably been as hot as the young guys we'd just seen, and Mom, who was about his age, would probably think he was hot now. He was the kind of guy you paid attention to in spite of how softly he spoke. Was he a bad guy, like Sam and Anya thought? Things and people were so different in Africa from what I was used to that I didn't feel like I could count on my intuition. I just couldn't tell.

The whole enclosure was called a *boma*, Jamison was saying, and the fence around it was always made of thorny branches. The fence did two things: keep the village's cattle and other animals in at night, and keep the lions and other wild animals out.

So that was why it looked and smelled like a barnyard. It actually *was* a barnyard all night long.

"I have asked our warriors to perform a traditional jumping contest," Jamison said, gesturing with one of his smiles toward the row of young men.

Suddenly one of the guys who'd been standing there yelled, and the next second he was three feet off the ground. Then another one shouted and jumped, and another and another. One by one they jumped into the air, so high it was almost unbelievable.

I couldn't take my eyes off them—not because of how good-looking they were, but because of how high they jumped. I realized that my mouth was hanging open again, and I shut it with a snap.

"Think of the muscles that takes!" I said at last. "If they had a standing high jump in the Olympics, one of these guys would win for sure."

Lucas was too busy taking pictures to answer.

"Two of these warriors are my sons," Jamison said, proudly gesturing toward two of the hot guys with the jewelry and fancy hairdos. One wore his hair in a bun and was just a tiny bit stockier than most of the other warriors. But the other was probably the hottest guy of all. He had especially broad shoulders, and his hair went halfway down his back. I wondered if American women ever completely fell for these guys and married them. I wouldn't have been surprised.

When they were finished with the jumping contest, the warriors showed us the scars on their legs. Each one had the same complicated pattern of scars on one thigh. Jamison explained that these were burn marks, made in a coming of age ceremony. The scars reminded me of what Lucas had said, that painful things were done to young men, but they had to not show any pain. I thought they must be incredibly brave.

Maybe a dozen women and children had lined up to have Lucas take their pictures, and a few of the smallest children sat in the mud and dung in front of them.

Almost all the women were wearing colorful robes underneath, and another layer of a different piece of fabric over that, tied around the neck to make a kind of cape.

The young men who'd been in the jumping ceremony had smiled and seemed happy, but the women and children had more sober expressions. I remembered the laughing children we'd seen coming out of the school in Narok in their pink and gray uniforms. These kids didn't seem nearly so carefree. I wasn't sure exactly what day of the week it was—it was hard to keep track when we'd spent so much time in an airplane—but I knew it was a weekday. Why weren't they in school? I thought of asking, but I wondered if having them home from school was part of their tradition, and I didn't want to be disrespectful.

When Lucas was finished taking pictures, Jamison led us to a hut that was a little larger than the others in the compound. "This is where my family and I live," he said. "You see we live very simply."

He moved the cloth away from the doorway and Lucas and I had a look. We probably had a longer time to see inside than most visitors would, because while we were standing there, one of Jamison's sons came up behind us and talked with his dad about something.

What we could see of the hut did seem very simple. A few tin dishes on a bench, a large tin bucket in one corner, three beds, and a bunch of thick branches stuck together somehow to make another bench. I didn't want to think about what they used to stick it together.

I wouldn't have noticed the most interesting thing about the hut if Lucas, with her photographic brain, hadn't told me what to look for. "That's weird," she muttered. "This room doesn't go back as far as it should."

"Really?" I asked in a soft voice.

She nodded, and breathed back, "This space is smaller than the hut is on the outside."

But there was no door into another room. So if there

was space behind the room's back wall, how did people get in and out?

Jamison's voice behind us said, "Come, girls. Let's move on."

"Things that make you go *hmm*," Lucas muttered, and turned to follow him.

19

Lucas Gets a Clue

The next minute Jamison took a few steps away from the house and started lecturing us again about how important animals had always been to the Maasai culture. He told us how hard life was for them since the drought, and that they now had to sell other things besides their animals in order to buy food from other places.

While he talked he led us to an opening into another whole area of the *boma*. In this part, the fence was lined with tables of jewelry and masks and cloth wall hangings and a bunch of other gift things.

Jamison had timed everything perfectly. Four vans, all of them named Superior Safaris, had pulled up at the front gate, and what seemed like dozens of people were pouring out. He gestured with his arm to get Lucas and me to go inside, then hurried away to lecture the next group of tourists.

There were probably ten more tourists inside the gift shop area, each one with their own special sales clerk. One of the clerks was just finishing up with a customer when we walked in. It was one of Jamison's sons. The hot one.

He had small braids in front of each of his ears. The rest of his hair was in tiny braids that went halfway to his waist. All the braids had beads and metal things in them.

This sounds dorky, but it wasn't. As he walked to us, shoulders and chin high, taking long strides with his bare feet, I noticed again how good-looking he was.

When he turned to lead us to one of the tables, Lucas took a glance at him, her eyes got big, and she waggled her head just the smallest amount, as if to say, "What a hunk."

Then she mouthed something that looked like, "Play along." I wasn't sure what was going on. Was she going to put the moves on this guy?

But it was something completely different. She pulled up beside him, with me following behind. I heard her say in a flirty voice, "Oh, I just love beadwork! I have to get a necklace for my mom and one for me, and maybe some bracelets."

This totally surprised me. For one thing, Lucas wasn't the flirty voice type. At least not with a total stranger. For another, I couldn't imagine either Lucas *or* her mother ever wearing African beadwork: Lucas never wore any kind of jewelry, and Camellia mostly liked things that sparkled and cost tons of money.

But Lucas went at the buying hot and heavy. She kept her eyes mostly on the warrior, grabbed some necklaces and bracelets, and picked up a short spear with a beaded handle.

"How much will all this be?" she asked, a little breathlessly. If I had thought she was serious about the flirting, I would have felt like rolling my eyes. But I figured there was something else going on.

"Fifty dollars American." All through the trip, the Kenyans we'd met seemed to like to be paid in American money.

Fifty dollars was a very high price for what she had. But instead of bargaining, which we knew we were supposed to do when we were in Kenya, Lucas gave him an adoring smile and said, "I'll take it."

She paid, took her bag of stuff, thanked him, turned to me, and said, "Kari, don't hurry. I'll just go into the other part of the *boma* and take some more pictures while I wait. I know how picky you are."

The warrior looked as surprised as I felt that she was leaving us. Normally, even if she didn't have a crush on a sales guy, Lucas would have stayed with me to see what I bought. She was obviously up to something.

Still looking confused, the guy turned to me. Behind him I saw Lucas disappear quickly into the other part of the *boma*.

I smiled at him, trying for the same adoring look Lucas had used. "What is your name?" I was stalling, trying to figure out what was going on.

"My name is Takeshi, but you may call me Marcus."

"I like Takeshi better, if you don't mind. My name is Kari. I like African names. Is that your brother over there?" I nodded my head at another person selling gifts.

"Yes, that is my brother. His Christian name is Norton, but his African name is Sunte."

I wasn't really thinking about the brothers. I was thinking about Lucas.

It took me only a few seconds to figure it out. You didn't have to be Einstein to know that what she wanted to take a picture of was the back of Jamison's hut. It also wasn't very hard to understand why she thought I needed to keep Takeshi busy. Even fearless Lucas, Lucas the Lionheart, must have realized that if something fishy was going on in Jamison's village, getting caught taking pictures of the secret entrance to the place where he and his family lived could get her into Very Big Trouble. And if Takeshi went back into the other part of the *boma* and she wasn't visible, he might start wondering just exactly where she had gone.

I felt torn in two. Half of me wanted to keep Takeshi in the gift area, half of me wanted to check on Lucas. My mouth went dry and I had a tight feeling in my chest.

"Um, right," I said, still stalling and trying not to look too panicked.

Lucas was trusting me to keep Takeshi busy, so that's what I would do. I took a deep breath. "It will probably take me a little while. My friend is right. I'm super picky."

While I was looking at the gifts, I got a good glance at Sunte out of the corner of my eye. He wasn't as good looking as his brother, although I had the feeling that, of the two, he was the boss. His hair was done up in a bun in back that included silver strands along with the hair, and he wore a complicated headband with silver discs dangling all around. He had a beaded necklace and a bracelet around the upper part of his arm that was made of beads and silver. He was solid, with big muscles. As the old saying goes, I thought he looked like the kind of guy you wouldn't want to meet alone in a dark alley.

As I fiddled around looking at one table of souvenirs and then another, I got more and more nervous. I kept thinking, *What is Lucas doing right now? Has anybody seen her?* It was all I could do not to run over to the gateway to the rest of the *boma* and take a peek.

Eventually a couple more tourists showed up for Takeshi to take care of. I quick made my final decision, did a little bargaining, said thank you, and took off.

I hadn't heard any shouting or actual screams, and that seemed like a good sign.

When I got back into the other section of the *boma*, another big group of tourists had arrived, and now people were everywhere. If that wasn't enough, a group of about fifteen or sixteen was standing in front of Jamison's hut, asking him questions about Maasai life. I wondered how long they'd been there, and how long it would take before they moved on.

With luck, Lucas had figured out a way to get her photo and was now completely finished, standing by the van and chatting with Bernard. If she was still in back of the hut, she was stuck. There was no way she could have come out in either direction without being seen by somebody.

I wandered out into the middle of the barnyard area where I could get a glimpse of Bernard's van on the other side of the open gate, hoping to see her, and my heart fell. Bernard was leaning against the van's passenger door, talking to another driver. I had a clear view through the van's windows, and there was absolutely no silhouette of a head inside.

Meep. Now what?

I had to think of something, and I had to have *time* to think of it. I didn't have a camera, and I didn't have any reason to stick around there since I'd already heard what Jamison had to say about the Maasai life. My heart was pounding so hard it hurt, and I was squeezing my fists until the nails dug into my palms.

What could I do to stay there and think a minute? My mind went blank. Suddenly I thought of the old shoe-tying trick. Okay, so I wasn't wearing shoes that tied. I found a place where there was no fresh manure, dropped to one knee, and pretended to adjust the strap on my sandal.

Head down, I looked at the space between the huts. Sure enough, as I watched, I saw Lucas take a quick peek out from around Jamison's back wall, mouth the word *Help!*, and disappear again.

I looked around at the other tourists, but nobody else seemed to have spotted her.

Help?! How could I help? I racked my brain, trying to come up with something I could do.

Anything.

All I could come up with was nothing.

I switched knees and started fiddling with the other sandal, my hands sweating now so that my fingers slipped on the leather. I took my lip between my teeth and bit it until it hurt.

My mind swirled around. What should I do? What should I do?

I stood up and spent as long as I possibly could to wipe the dirt off my knees, still playing for time. Should I pretend to faint? No, then I'd have to fall onto the ground. I thought of what was on the ground. Yech! Unless I got completely desperate, that was out. Should I run out the front gate and get Bernard to honk his horn really loud? Should I—

Suddenly I had an idea. I could shout, make a scene. But what about?

Then something came back to me, something from

the mini-lecture Lucas had given about the Maasai people and their culture while we were at the front gate.

I gritted my teeth and rolled my eyes. I was not going to like this. I hate even being noticed, and being the center of attention for a bunch of adults was about as appealing as the smell inside the *boma*. But it beat pretending to faint and having to fall down in the manure.

I started trotting across the compound. "Mr. Jamison! Mr. Jamison!" I yelled, even waving one arm, if you can believe that. Calling him Mister like that, like I would with a teacher, made me feel like a character in a rerun of some ancient sitcom.

He turned to me, and I yelled, "Somebody told me that Maasai villages have heads of lions they've killed that they use in ceremonies!" By this time, I'd gotten up to him, but I kept on talking in a loud voice as if I was super excited. "If this village has any of those lion heads, could we see one?"

Jamison said something to a young boy who was standing nearby, and I took that moment to look around, moving only my eyeballs. Sure enough, the heads of pretty much everybody in the compound had turned in our direction. Close by on my left, a voice said, "The head of a real lion!?" and behind me, someone said, "I wonder what kind of ceremony."

"I've sent a boy to fetch one of our ceremonial heads," Jamison said, and around me I heard the buzz of a lot of people talking.

The kid was back in seconds, wearing the lion head. It was way more awesome than I would have imagined. It was the head of a male lion, with a mane. Its chin rested on the shoulders of the boy, and the mouth stretched so wide that the kid's face was completely visible between the jaws. There was a bunch of *oohs* and *aahs*, and the sound of cameras clicking.

"Oh, Mr. Jamison, that is so cool!" I said. "Thank you for letting us see that." I gave him the best smile I could come up with and handed him a five dollar tip, and the minute his back was turned, I took off to where Lucas was calmly waiting for me in the van.

I blew out a breath. Those pictures had better be meeping worth it.

She waited until Bernard had slid the door closed behind me and was walking around the van, then muttered, "I got some awesome shots!"

"I hope so," I said back, and gave her a dirty look.

When Bernard opened the driver's side door, she said, "Come over here for a second, Kari. Take a look at these pictures."

I knelt in the aisle beside her seat and looked at the screen on Lucas's camera. The picture was of a narrow passage, maybe four feet wide, between the *boma* fence and what must have been Jamison's hut.

She clicked, and the next picture was a close-up of the fence. It was definitely a side view, but I could see the thorn tree branches and, right in the middle, a piece of leather maybe two inches high and five inches wide, one end nailed to one of the branches and the other end to the other branch.

"Look at the way they make hinges using leather," she said, her voice sounding casual, as if she was describing the hinges on the gate from the *boma* into the gift area. *I* knew it was a gate in the fence behind Jamison's hut.

"Interesting," I said, playing along.

"That's the one at the top. There was another one just like it at the bottom. Here's how they fasten it shut."

The next picture showed a thick stick shoved through leather straps nailed to the thorn tree branches.

Lucas clicked the camera again, and now I was looking at a big door in a mud wall.

"Great shot of that jumping contest!" I said.

"This one"—another click—"is the best of all." It was a clear picture of some tire tracks in the mud.

"It would be interesting to find out what kind of animal made those tracks," I said.

I got back up into my seat and fastened my seat belt, then wrestled around in my bag. "Let me show you the things I got from the gift shop. I got these cool bracelets, and look at this mask!"

But all the time I was wondering what was in the vehicle that came and went through the gate and unloaded into the back of Jamison's hut.

20

The Meaning of the Tracks

The crew from the dig site had obviously gotten home before we did, because we met Uncle Geoff as he came out of the lodge building. On our way to the tent we showed him the things we'd bought in the Maasai gift shop.

When we got to the tent, I said, "We'll talk about the village at dinner, when Professor Wanjohi is there. Right now I just want to jump in the shower."

"I've always wondered about all these people who jump in the shower," Uncle Geoff said. "You wouldn't think it would be really safe. One might so easily slip. Me, I just stand there and scrub and let the water run over me."

"Smart meep," I said.

Once the tent flap was zipped behind us, getting into the shower and either jumping there or standing still and scrubbing was not what we were thinking about the most.

The minute we were alone, Lucas whispered, "Those tracks in my picture are from a Land Rover. I checked it out in the parking lot."

"Well, that narrows it down a *little*," I said in a low voice. "Show me those pictures again. I want to get a better look."

We sat down on the bed next to each other and stared at the screen on her camera. "Okay," I said, as she clicked through the shots, "what we have here is a gate in the *boma* behind Jamison's hut big enough to drive a vehicle through. Some tracks showing that that's what was happening. And a door into the back of Jamison's house where the vehicle loaded or unloaded something. Right?"

Lucas nodded.

"And it's a Land Rover."

She nodded again. This was the kind of thing I'd gotten used to taking her word for. "I noticed that most of the Land Rovers had tires that were a lot alike. But we should probably take a look at the ones in the parking lot to see if it's one of them. I mean, there have to be little differences in the tires—some newer, some older, that kind of thing."

I sighed, wondering how many thousands of Land Rovers there were on the Masai Mara at that very minute. But I knew Lucas was enthused, so instead of throwing cold water on things, I said, "This secret space at the back of Jamison's hut would be a great place to store the things they took from the cave."

She nodded. "If that's what it's used for, it would mean Jamison or someone in his family has found another entrance to the cave, just like Sam thought. They dig the artifacts out, take them to Jamison's place, and these"— she pointed at the tire tracks—"are from the vehicle that picks them up and takes them to Nairobi."

I got a shiver of excitement. Then suddenly I had another thought, and the excitement went away.

"What if the tracks are made by the vehicle that's used to pick up the crafts made at the neighboring Maasai villages and deliver them to the gift shop?"

Lucas thought about that for a minute. "Why would the gate be hidden? I mean, if it was just a normal delivery, wouldn't they drive through the front gate and right into the gift shop area?"

I sucked in my lips, considering this. "If the crafts actually are unloaded into the back of Jamison's hut, then it seems to me that having the door in an almost invisible place like this could be the way they keep other people in the village from knowing what's going on."

"Like, they might store both the crafts *and* the artifacts there, and having the door where it is lets them take the artifacts away without anyone seeing them, or getting suspicious."

I nodded. "That's what I was thinking. We need to find out from Sam and Anya if they know who goes to pick up the arts and crafts. Do you think one of them will come here, or will they contact us a different way?"

Lucas shrugged. "We didn't talk about that."

I shook my head. "Maybe we'd better just be natural about it and do what we'd do if we weren't waiting for them."

"Okay, then if you don't mind, I'm going to get in the shower and scrub and let the water run over me," Lucas said. "When I'm finished—"

"I'll get in and jump," I said.

Anya had perfect timing. Lucas had finished dressing and I was just putting on my sandals when we heard her voice outside. "Hello," she called out. "I'm here with the drinks you ordered."

We hadn't ordered any drinks, but it was a brilliant way for her to get inside our tent.

"Did you have an interesting day?" she asked, handing Lucas her usual Coke and me my usual mango juice. Then, in a soft voice that couldn't be heard outside the tent, she added, "Did everything go okay?"

"We got to the village, and everything went fine," Lucas said.

If you didn't count Lucas almost getting trapped, I thought.

When she finished signing the receipt for the drinks, Lucas handed Anya her camera. "Take a look at the photos I got. I took these behind Jamison's hut," she said.

Anya flipped through the pictures quickly, not stopping on any of them long enough to figure out what they meant. "I cannot really stay and talk about this right now," she said when she handed the camera back. "Can you meet us again tonight?"

"Same time, same place?" I asked.

She nodded.

Lucas held out a dollar bill as a tip.

"I will not take a tip for drinks you did not order," Anya said with a smile. She lifted the flap, looked around, and stepped outside.

When she'd gone, Lucas said, "Let's go look at the tracks the Land Rovers make."

The parking lot was a dirt and gravel area inside the brick wall that ran around the complex, with a huge metal gate that was kept closed except when the vehicles were coming and going. A high wooden fence with short blooming bushes around the bottom of it separated the lot from the rest of the complex. I figured the fence was probably there because when it was crowded with vans and Land Rovers the lot was kind of ugly, and everything else about the complex was beautiful.

By the time we got there, most or maybe all of the

safari groups had come back for the evening. Of the total twenty vehicles, nine were Land Rovers. Fortunately for us, absolutely nobody was around. The tracks were all crisscrossed, but most of them had the little differences Lucas had thought they would. If you concentrated, you could follow them to the vehicle that made them.

Eventually the two of us separated, each of us taking one side of the driveway that led into the parking area. I had the camera with the picture on it, because Lucas carried the picture around in her head.

We'd probably looked for a good five minutes when I said, "Lucas, come over here."

I pointed toward a particular set of tracks and, trying to keep the excitement out of my voice, said, "These are the ones, aren't they." It was more a statement than a question, because the answer seemed obvious.

I handed Lucas the camera so we could make sure. She stooped on one knee, looked closely at the track I was talking about, stood up, and whispered, "This is it, all right. Now who does it belong to?"

There were five Land Rovers on my side of the driveway. I won't go into all of our tracking, but finally we found the one whose tires matched the picture from behind Jamison's hut.

When we'd picked it out for sure, Lucas said, "It's Prosper's."

"How do you know?"

"The license plate." Of course, she would have it memorized. She aimed her camera where she could photograph both the tracks and the license plate at the same time, and clicked.

There was a sound behind us. We both turned, and there was Prosper, stepping from the path onto the dust and gravel of the parking lot.

How long had he been there? And what had he heard?

21

The Other Man in Maria's Life

I sucked in my breath, and my heart jumped so hard inside my chest that it actually hurt. Prosper's eyes were half closed, as if he was suspicious. Who could blame him? Even if he hadn't been listening in on what we'd said, he'd probably seen us taking pictures of his Land Rover. That would give the nicest guy in the world a reason to wonder what we were up to. But between Bernard's attitude when I talked about Prosper and now finding out that his vehicle made the tracks behind the hut where Jamison and his family lived, I was more and more sure he *wasn't* a nice guy. Which made being caught like this a little bit scary.

Lucas the Lionheart managed to say hello to him in a casual sounding voice. All he did was nod back.

"Not good," she muttered when we were away from him.

"You got that right," I said. "Let's hope that all he does is pick up crafts and drive them to Jamison's village."

"I wonder if he's staring at us," Lucas said as we got to the top of the hill. Her head moved to glance over her shoulder.

"No, Lucas—"

"Don't worry," she said. "He's just meeting some guy."

I took a look for myself. He was chatting away with a guy who reminded me of Mike Myers, the guy who played Austin Powers. "I wonder who it is," I said.

"*I'm* wondering why they decided to meet in the parking lot."

"Does seem kind of strange, doesn't it?"

We got back to our tent just in time to meet Uncle Geoff for dinner. As we walked to the dining room, I asked how the work had gone at the dig after we'd left.

He looked at me. "A whole lot better than it would have gone if you hadn't said what you did about Britt. Thanks, kiddo."

"I have a question for you," I said.

"Shoot."

"How did it feel to have Maria madly in love with you?"

My question made both Lucas and me burst out laughing.

Uncle Geoff's face turned pink, and he said, "It was quite a strain. I don't know what I did to deserve the honor, or the curse, or whatever it is."

"Was she bragging again today?"

"She was trying to be subtle, of course, but basically she was bragging. My one consolation is that Charlie says she's pretentious pretty much all the time. It's only marginally worse with me around.

"What worries me," he continued, "is that I understand she already *has* a man in her life. The head pilot for the company that offers the balloon safaris over the Masai Mara. Guy named Reggie."

Lucas and I looked at each other, but Uncle Geoff must not have noticed, because he kept on talking. "When you take your ride, he'll probably be at the helm, if balloons can be said to have helms. I'm not particularly excited about being cast as the Other Man in Maria's life, especially given the fact that I have absolutely zero interest in her. Romantically, that is."

We had to step off the sidewalk onto the grass to make room for a couple that was walking toward us.

"Can we go sit on that bench?" Lucas asked.

Uncle Geoff nodded. He looked a little bewildered, which was how I felt, too.

When we sat down, Lucas said, "It's probably only fair for you to know that she's using you to try to make Reggie jealous."

I didn't meeping believe this. Didn't she know how much trouble we were going to be in if she told him about spying at Maria's tent? I had a sudden vision of the Ghost of Mom if she found out we'd been sneaking around the campsite late at night. This time she was pacing and yelling.

But trust Lucas to put the best spin possible on it. "We took a little walk after dinner last night down to the end of the path and back. And when we were walking past Maria's tent, we overheard something she said on her phone."

Uncle Geoff got a stern look on his face. Before he could give us a lecture about how we shouldn't be listening in to private conversations, Lucas said, "We couldn't have passed her tent without hearing it. She wasn't talking softly or anything, and all her tent windows were unzipped." Which wasn't exactly a lie.

Uncle Geoff raised an eyebrow to show he didn't trust Lucas's story absolutely, but so far so good on the lecture. I let out a breath. I hadn't even known I'd been holding it.

"Anyway," Lucas continued, "it must have been the balloon pilot, because she called him Reggie. She was talking about you to try to make him jealous."

Now both of Uncle Geoff's eyebrows were up, and I didn't think it was because he didn't believe our story.

"What did she say?"

Lucas, with her incredible memory, was always able to quote perfectly. "She said, 'Reggie, I didn't say there was anything between us. Yet. I've just said that you now have a bit of competition to keep you on your toes.' Then he said something, and she said she liked his response, and maybe this would make him show up on time when he came to dinner here, and that would be in contrast to his past behavior."

"Anything else?" Uncle Geoff asked, scratching his cheek.

I was about to say that we hadn't heard anything else about him, but Lucas beat me to it and said, "By that time we'd passed the tent." Which wasn't exactly true, but at least kept us out of trouble.

"Thanks for letting me know," Uncle Geoff said after a few seconds of silence. "In that case, I'm very glad I'm not going on the balloon ride with you. If he's the jealous type, it could be a very quick trip down for me from the balloon to the ground, with a very abrupt ending."

Being reminded of the meeping balloon ride sent my heart into my stomach again. That quick trip with the abrupt ending was exactly the kind of thing that scared me every time I thought about it.

22

Candelabra Trees, Part Two

Going back to the candelabra trees was more fun this time because we knew where we were going. The night sounds were familiar to us now, and so were the lights by the path, and even the smell of the flowers, which seemed to be almost stronger at night than it was in the daytime. And we knew who was staying in some of the tents. It was like we were getting to know the neighborhood, and the bench in front of the candelabra trees was our secret place.

Anya and Sam were waiting for us, just like they'd been before.

We'd only just sat down and hadn't said much more than hello before Anya said, "I told Sam you had some good pictures from the Maasai village."

"I think if we smush in, we can all fit on the bench," I said, and scooted over to the far edge.

"You can see the pictures better if you'll let me sit

between the two of you," Lucas said to Sam and Anya.

When we got settled, she held the camera screen out at arm's length and started flicking through the photos again. "Okay, this is Jamison's back door," she said. "By the way, I checked it out. Jamison's was the only hut that had a door in the back. At least on that side of the *boma*."

She flicked through slowly. "This one is the gate in the *boma* wall that's only about half a car length behind Jamison's back door. These are the hinges. This one is the fastener on the gate. These are tracks in the dust from where the Land Rover came through and backed up to Jamison's house.

"Here's the really interesting part." She flicked to the last photo and held the camera for the two of them to see. "That's a picture of the tracks made by Prosper's Land Rover."

She went back to the picture from behind the hut. "See? The tracks match exactly. We went out to the parking lot before dinner and checked out all the vehicles that were there. Prosper's was the only one that matched exactly."

She lowered the camera to her lap. "Do you know if Prosper goes around to the Maasai villages to collect the crafts that are sold in Jamison's village?"

Sam nodded. "Yes, he is the one. He does it to make extra money."

"Could you ask—" I broke off. "I've forgotten the

name of your Maasai friend, the one who comes every morning."

"Koyati," Anya said.

"Could you ask Koyati about the gate? I mean, Lucas and I think it would be weird if the crafts from other villages were delivered through this back gate. If the crafts come in through the main gate, what's this back gate used for? If this is where Jamison delivers the crafts, why is it in such a secret place?"

"Yeah," Lucas said. "Is it in back of Jamison's hut so that no one in the village can see what comes in and what goes out?"

Sam and Anya looked at each other, thinking about this. Finally Sam turned to us. "I will ask Koyati what he can find out. You believe that Prosper may be the person who transports the artifacts from Jamison's village, is that correct?"

"Yes," Lucas said, "but we know that he has to stay here and work every day, or almost every day. So he can't be the one taking the rocks and things to Nairobi. There has to be a third person."

"We saw him with someone in the parking lot before dinner," I said. "Maybe that was the third person. We thought it was odd that he'd be meeting with somebody there."

Sam shook his head. "It is not really unusual. Prosper does many small jobs for people, and I have often seen him making arrangements in the parking lot."

"Like what kind of jobs?" I asked.

Sam shrugged. "Well, for example, the drinks at the bar here are quite expensive. So sometimes a guest will ask Prosper to go into one of the towns nearby and get a bottle of something they could drink in their tent for many dollars less than they would spend in the bar."

Anya added, "This is against the lodge rules, although everyone knows it goes on. Still, it would not be good to make the arrangements in the open, so Prosper meets the guest in the parking lot where they are not likely to be seen."

I looked at Lucas. "Meep!" I said, wrinkling my nose. "So the guy with him could be almost anybody."

"Yes, it is not necessarily an accomplice in the crime. But your idea that Prosper might have something to do with the smuggling is very intriguing," Sam said. "I will ask around to see if anyone knows of a connection between Jamison and Prosper."

"We'll keep our eyes and ears open," Lucas said.

"Please do not do any dangerous things," Anya said. "It would be terrible if something happened to you. I would feel responsible. Promise me." The Ghost of Mom now seemed to have the ability to channel her voice through Anya.

I looked at Lucas. She was the risk taker. She said, "Okay, we promise. No dangerous things."

I could see only one of her hands. I wondered if she was crossing her fingers on the other.

23

Lucas Makes a Confession

It was nearly eleven when Lucas and I got back to our tent. We hadn't seen anyone on the path, and we changed into our pajamas silently in the dark so no one would know we'd been out.

I was super tired and ready to go to sleep the minute I got horizontal. But as we crawled into our beds, Lucas whispered, "Can I be honest and tell you something and not have you get mad at me?"

This was so not like Lucas that I hardly knew what to say. "Yeah, shoot," I whispered back.

"Promise you won't yell at me."

"I can't believe you're saying this. What would be so bad that I'd yell at you? And yeah, I promise, because if I yelled, I'd wake up the whole camp."

Lucas was quiet for a minute. Whatever she was going to tell me had to be pretty big stuff.

Finally she let out a huge sigh and said, "I don't really

care about the missing artifacts. At least not as much as you do."

She'd been right. It took all my strength not to yell at her. I sucked my lips between my teeth and bit on them to keep my mouth shut.

"Remember that little lecture your uncle gave us?" she continued. "The one where he was telling us why looting an archaeological site was bad?"

"Yeah?" I grunted.

"Well, even though I got what he was saying, I couldn't get all excited about the missing artifacts. I mean, what I don't get is, even when the professional archaeologists dig up a site, they leave more than half of what's there still in the ground. So why does the rest of the stuff matter?"

I stayed quiet. It was way too late at night to get in an argument, especially since I didn't even know where to start. How could you not care about losing ancient clues about the way people lived in prehistory, way before anything was ever written down? How could you not care if a country's natural treasures were taken away by somebody who only wanted them for the money they were worth?

"I know, I know," she said, as if she was reading my mind. "Before we came on this trip you were always going on and on about archaeology and prehistoric treasures and the history of people who lived way back thousands of years ago and all that."

Did I really go on and on about archaeology? And did

I go on about it the way she went on about Africa? Did I give mini-lectures?

"I thought that once I went to the dig site I might completely change my mind," she said. "But I didn't. At least, not a lot."

I tried to think of something to say to her either about her not caring about the artifacts or about me lecturing her, but I was too tired to think of anything good.

Finally I came up with, "So if you don't care about the treasures, why were you so interested in solving the mystery? I mean, before we met Anya and everything?"

"Just because it *was* a mystery."

"Why are you telling me this at eleven o'clock at night?"

"Because once I knew that Bernard could be arrested, I *really* began to care about finding the people who did it. Now it's not just about the rocks and things anymore. It's about Bernard and Anya and Sam."

I thought she'd already said something like that the night before. But I didn't bring it up. Instead, I just said, "Yeah?"

"I'm really excited now, because I feel like we're making real progress in solving the crime."

I didn't say anything. My eyes felt heavier and heavier.

"Okay, I just wanted to be honest with you."

"That's good . . . I guess," I said.

And that's the last thing I remembered until morning.

24

The Circle of Life

We had another game drive the next day, and I was a little surprised that seeing even the same kind of animals we'd seen on our earlier trips still felt amazing. The elephants, the zebras, the giraffes, the wildebeest, all the kinds of antelope—being there with them was completely awesome. We also saw our first family of warthogs, right there by the side of the road, practically inches away from us. They were so ugly they were cute.

There were also some important new things. One was after lunch, when Bernard stopped the car, raised the roof, and said, "Look up on top of that hill over there."

I saw something moving but couldn't tell what it was until I used my binoculars. With them, I could see it was a lion with her teeth clamped around a huge piece of bloody carcass, dragging it along on the ground.

"Wow! A real live lion!" Lucas said.

"Kind of gross, though," I said, following the animal

with my binoculars as she moved across the horizon. "I guess hunting animals is . . . what lions do."

"You are right, Kari," Bernard said. "Her cubs must be over the hill. She is taking food for the family to eat. Look over there."

We both stood up and looked where Bernard had pointed. "Hyenas!" Lucas said.

"And overhead."

Four huge vultures were circling.

"The hyenas will take whatever is left after the lions are done with it, and the vultures will clean up after the hyenas," Bernard said. We sat back down and he lowered the roof.

I thought of what we'd seen. An hour before, what the lioness was dragging around now had been a beautiful impala with those graceful horns, or a scampering Tommy, or maybe a little zebra. Now this animal was dead and had become food for the lioness and her cubs, and for the hyenas and for the vultures. Food that helped them stay alive. This was the real Circle of Life, and it wasn't cute and cuddly, but it was the way Mother Nature meant it to be.

We had box lunches along that day. Bernard asked us if we would like to go to a place with a picnic table, or would rather eat at a place where we would be surrounded by birds "singing like crazy." Well, duh, of course we picked the place with the birds.

Lucas and I sat inside the sliding door to the back of the van, our feet dangling, and Bernard sat perched on the front passenger seat facing out the open door. A flock of the brilliant blue birds I'd seen on our way to the restroom in the Rift Valley gathered at our feet to eat the crumbs from our sandwiches and potato chips and cookies. I'd never seen anything in nature that was quite that electric blue color, not even a flower. Bernard said they were called splendid starlings, and I thought splendid was the word for them.

And he'd been right with the "singing like crazy" business. Although we could see only a few of them, we were surrounded by all kinds of birds singing at the top of their lungs. And what made it interesting enough to tell about was that the birds didn't sound the same as they did at home. In Minnesota, we get birds that sing mostly soprano, and maybe a little alto. In Africa, the birds sing all the parts, all the way down to bass.

"It's the African Symphony Orchestra and Choral Ensemble," I said.

Lucas added, "This may be their version of the 'Hallelujah' chorus." Except for that, the three of us were mostly quiet. I ate my cookie and listened to the birds, sniffed the air smelling of plants and flowers, and watched the starlings on the ground below us and a beautiful spotted bird singing away in a nearby tree.

"It seems so peaceful here," I said at last. "Like if

you just stayed here and didn't move, nothing bad could happen to you."

I let a second of silence pass, then added, "*Hmph.*" The sound said that I knew that this wasn't true, that for the animals, nowhere was safe as long as there were predators around.

I glanced up and happened to catch an expression I'd never seen on Bernard's face. His lips were tight together, his nostrils flared, and his eyes were aimed into the distance, but not as if he was seeing anything there. It was the closest I'd seen to anything bitter or truly unhappy on his face.

That was when I knew that he, too, was waiting for the other shoe to drop.

That afternoon we came around a corner and saw an enormous animal in the middle of the road, looking straight at us. He was black, with horns that stuck way out to the side and curled up, and he had the same mean look I'd seen on the faces of bulls when Mom and I went to a rodeo when we were on vacation in the Black Hills in South Dakota.

"That's a cape buffalo," Bernard said.

He pulled on the handbrake. "If we try to keep going, he'll think we're an aggressor, and he's big enough to charge us and tip the van over." He settled back on his seat and folded his arms. "We're not going anywhere until *he* goes somewhere."

"Hey, we've forgotten to think about the Big Five!" Lucas said. "With the lion and the cape buffalo, we've seen two of them today!"

"You may count the lion if you wish, Lucas," Bernard said, "but as your safari guide, I will not be satisfied until you get a much better look. There are many lions in the Masai Mara. We usually see males and females sitting together by the side of the road looking peaceful. I am very surprised we haven't seen one up till now. I expect you will get a closer view sometime very soon."

"That would be so awesome!" Lucas said.

"Totally!" I added.

Bernard was right. We would be close to a lion soon. Much, much closer than we'd ever wanted to be, and in a situation none of us could have imagined.

25

Fears, and an Almost Fight

At dinner, Professor Wanjohi said that the policemen he'd been dealing with about the smuggling hadn't made a good impression on him. He didn't think anyone was actually investigating the crime at all. So he'd called a high-up police inspector guy from Mombasa whom he had worked with before, and trusted. The inspector, who the professor called Raza, said he'd come out himself as soon as he finished the case he was working on. He was going to try to make it out within the next two days.

I wondered if the professor thought that the police he'd dealt with were corrupt. If they were, it would be good to have someone around who really cared about solving the crime. I hoped that by the time the inspector came, Lucas and I would have some clues to give him.

After the business with the Land Rover's tires, Lucas and I couldn't help glancing over at Prosper every so often as we ate.

Once I looked in his direction at the same time someone at his table must have cracked a joke, because everyone sitting there except Prosper laughed.

I poked Lucas with my elbow to make sure she saw what was going on.

As we watched, Prosper looked at the guys sitting around him, his eyes half closed, reached for a piece of bread, took a bite, and chewed. Someone said something that must have added to the joke, because there was another wave of laughter. Prosper took another bite of bread, not cracking a smile.

Charlie, who had seen us watching, said, "Prosper doesn't laugh at my jokes, either."

"What do you think of him?" Lucas asked.

"I never trust anyone who lacks a sense of humor." His mustache twitched, but I wasn't sure this was a total joke. Maybe that was all that was wrong with Prosper—he didn't have a sense of humor. But I thought from Charlie's tone of voice that he didn't have a completely good feeling about him. Maybe not any more than I did.

The really nice thing about being at the table with the others that night was that Maria was out with the balloon guy and we didn't have to listen to her obnoxious laugh.

When I muttered something about Maria being gone, Lucas muttered back, "I wonder if Reggie is as good looking as your uncle." I'd never heard her call Uncle Geoff good looking before. "I can't wait to check him out on the balloon ride tomorrow."

My stomach clutched up. The balloon ride. *You don't have to go, Kari. You don't have to go.*

If I wasn't going to go, I *was* going to have to tell Lucas about it pretty soon because the van that would take us out to where the balloon took off was scheduled to come at a quarter to five the next morning. I was pretty close to the deadline.

It occurred to me that I didn't like using the words *dead* and *balloon* so close together.

I made sure she and I were alone at the buffet table when it was time to choose our dessert courses.

"Um, Lucas?"

"Um, Kari?"

This was already not going well.

"Lucas, there's something I need to talk to you about and I have to do it fast."

She looked at me, a little surprised. "Animal, vegetable, or mineral?"

She does this to me all the time, and it makes me meeping nuts.

I closed my eyes for a second and tried not to lose my temper.

At last I opened my eyes, took a big breath, and said, "First, I don't really like it when you say that animal, vegetable, or mineral thing to me. And I'd love to explain that another time, but the important thing right now is that I don't think I want to go on the balloon ride tomorrow."

She turned away from the curried lamb and stared at me. "This is a joke, right?"

"Lucas, I've told you at least three times that I might not want to go on the balloon ride because I'm afraid of heights."

"I didn't think you were serious."

"Then why did you think I was saying it? Just for fun?"

"All the tourist Web sites say it's one of the best possible things to do when you're in Africa," she said. "You're not going to give it up just because you have this stupid fear, are you?"

This really made me mad. I pulled her around behind the dessert table where nobody was going this early in the dinner.

"Talk about a stupid fear!" I said, trying hard to keep my voice down. "At least my fear makes total sense. If I fell out of a balloon, I could die. But how about you and spiders?"

"Spiders can kill people!" she said.

"A few big nasty ones do. I'm not even sure we have any of those in Minnesota. You're afraid of even a teeny tiny daddy longlegs! Don't talk to me about a stupid fear! When you're willing to go outside and pick up the first spider you find and hold it in your hands long enough to count to three, then you get to talk to me about having a stupid fear. Until then, just—"

I closed my mouth about one sixteenth of a second before I told her to shut up. Which I knew would be dumb and end up getting us so totally mad at each other that we wouldn't be able to stay in the same tent together. We still had a week and a half to go. I didn't want to ruin our trip. Or our mystery.

I took a deep breath, walked over to the main courses, took a spoonful of rice, topped it off with chicken in tarragon cream sauce, and headed back to the table. I thought Lucas was behind me, but I didn't look. I totally didn't care.

When we both finished that course, Lucas nudged me and flicked her head toward the bathroom. "Come with me?" she said, making it a question.

I nodded and followed her.

There was a woman in there when we opened the door, and as we waited for her to leave we did the things people usually do in the bathroom, not to go into too much detail or anything.

When we were out of the stalls and washing our hands, Lucas said, "I'm sorry, Kari. I guess I didn't know how really scared you were of being up in the air."

"Well, I've told you often enough!" I said. I could hear that Ghost of Mom voice saying, *You've gone too far, Kari. You're getting an apology. Just keep your mouth shut and accept it.*

I sucked in my breath. "I'm sorry. I shouldn't have said that."

"No, you're right. I've been acting stupid. I was really off base when I insulted you like that."

As I've said before, one of the best things about Lucas is that when she's wrong, she admits it.

"I guess, when you compared it to spiders—well, I kind of get it now. So if you don't want to go up in the balloon, that's okay with me. I'll be fine without you. Seriously."

"Thanks for saying you're sorry, Lucas."

We stood there for a while without talking. I leaned my hands on the counter and looked at the two of us in the mirror. I thought about spiders and how, yes, there were spiders that could kill you, but most didn't. I thought about heights, and how there were some people who died because they fell off something. But mostly they didn't fall. In fact, in real life, I'd never known anybody who'd had that kind of thing happen to them, except, like, mountain climbers and people who were working on slanting roofs, and even a lot of the people who fell off roofs didn't die.

I closed my eyes and breathed for a minute, then turned to look at Lucas. "I've made up my mind. I'm going on that meeping balloon safari. Even if it *does* kill me."

26

Drama in the Parking Lot

We hadn't been back at the table more than a few seconds when suddenly the lights went out. I gasped. Just then I heard the beginning of a chant behind the kitchen door. The door swung open and out came Sam, carrying a big torch. Behind him was a long row of people singing and chanting some strange but really great African music. Their footsteps stomped and their bodies moved in time to the chant. The whole line was made up of people who worked at the lodge. All of them were in their tribal clothes—some wearing cloth that looked like animal skin, a few in *real* animal skin, which must have been hot in the warm room—and their faces painted. Two of the guys wore red Maasai robes, and some women had the kind of outfits and headdresses we'd seen in Nairobi.

Anya was right behind Sam, wearing a bright blue cropped top, a wraparound skirt made of cloth that looked like zebra skin, and a zebra-looking band around her head. A belt of wooden beads was draped around her bare waist and a column of short white lines had been painted on her cheekbones. She held a small drum in her hand that she tapped with a long bone.

She led the singing, dancing line around the room, and every so often she'd make this high sound, where she'd sing one long note and use her tongue or maybe just her throat to make it sound trembly. Together with the rest of the music, which was all in some native language, the whole thing seemed totally African.

It was absolutely awesome, and it was fun to see our friend Anya looking happy. She obviously liked what she was doing and was good at it. I thought that if she lived in America she'd probably be in some rock band or something.

We finished our desserts and stood up to go. The professor had gone to his tent early again to work on his research. Charlie and Uncle Geoff were taking off to have a nightcap in the bar when we heard a big commotion outside. Some guy shouted and we heard the sound of a woman's voice.

Charlie frowned. More shouting.

"Wait here. I'll go out and see what all the hubbub is about," he said.

"I'll go with you." Uncle Geoff looked at us. "Girls,

we'll be back in a few minutes." He took off after Charlie.

Lucas got up and headed after them. "Holy schmack. What do they think we are, helpless females?"

"Right. And they're Will Smith and sidekick," I said sarcastically as we scooted quickly through the lobby.

The next minute we were out of the building and running down the hill to the parking lot where the shouting was coming from. We joined the crowd that had gathered just inside the lot entrance.

The area was lit up with tall lamps like streetlights spaced around the fence. In the middle of it a guy in khaki pants, a camouflage jacket, and a beret was shoving someone into a big police van with lights on top. And the guy he was shoving was Bernard, now wearing handcuffs.

In the light of the van's headlights, another policeman shouted at Sam, who stood with his arm around Anya. She still wore the costume from the singing and dancing. Sam held up a hand, palm out, as if to get the cop to stop or quiet down. After slamming the van door behind Bernard, the other policeman came up and took over the shouting. When both cops finally shut up, Sam said something quietly, Anya added something, and the policemen shouted again. It wasn't in English, so we couldn't understand any of it.

Lucas and I walked around the front of the crowd to stand next to Uncle Geoff and Charlie.

"Why are those policemen yelling at Sam and Anya?" Lucas asked.

Uncle Geoff shook his head as if he didn't know. But a woman near us said, "I believe the young woman tried to keep them from putting handcuffs on the man in custody. And I think the young man was trying to keep her from being arrested."

Lucas and I looked at each other. I gulped. How could they arrest Anya?

Still shouting, one of the policemen shook his finger in Anya's face, finally stopped, and the two cops turned and got into the van. Anya kept her head up as they started the ignition, the glum expression on her face clear in the bright headlights. But the minute the vehicle backed through the wide open gate into the road, she began to cry, her shoulders heaving as she sobbed. Sam pulled her closer and said something into her ear.

A man in the crowd turned to the rest of us and asked, "Do you have any idea why he's been arrested?"

The people around us shook their heads.

But *we* knew. We knew perfectly well what it was about. All the yelling and commotion was the sound of the other shoe dropping.

27

Up, Up, and Away

A quarter after four came unbelievably early the next morning. Lucas and I splashed some water on our faces, brushed our teeth, pulled on clothes, and were down in the lodge by a little past four thirty. One of the staff members, a woman whose name badge said Lia, offered us cups of coffee. We both took one, even though Lucas and I don't like regular coffee, but we needed something to help wake us up. After we put in a lot of cream and sugar, it didn't taste so bad.

"Excuse me, Lia," I asked, "do you know anything about how Anya is?"

Lia shook her head. "After the police left I saw her walking with Sam toward the staff housing, but I didn't see her after that."

Once again I felt guilty about going out to enjoy tourist things while Anya and her family were having so much trouble. I thought of telling Lucas she should go without me and I'd stay at the lodge and find out what I could. But that would obviously look like I was trying to get out of going on the balloon ride, and after our almost fight the night before, I didn't want to do that. So I was stuck with going, whether I wanted to or not.

We weren't the only guests from the lodge who had signed up. A good-looking, well-dressed couple was waiting with us. They introduced themselves and said, in perfect English, that they were from Argentina.

The van with the balloon company's logo on the side came for us at four forty-five, exactly on schedule, and we all went outside in the pitch darkness and piled in.

I spent the first minutes thinking about Bernard being in jail, and from the glum expression on Lucas's face, I figured that was what she was thinking about, too. If the other couple knew anything about the scene that had taken place in the parking lot the night before, they didn't mention it.

We hadn't been under way for very long before the driver, a friendly young guy who said his name was Jeremiah, started telling us about the fancy breakfast we were going to have at the end of the balloon ride.

"The crew follows the balloon across country in their vehicles and sets up and serves breakfast near where it is able to land. If you look closely at the servers, you may see one you recognize." He smiled widely at me in the rearview mirror, and I guessed that I would see him at breakfast, too.

By the time we got to the launching place, it was just beginning to get light. As we pulled up, we saw an enormous red and gold balloon lying on its side partially inflated. Its colors almost exactly matched the orange and red strip of sky right above the horizon.

"Wow!" Lucas said. "It's gigantic!"

I didn't say anything. On the way out I'd thought a little bit about staying in my day, but now the sight of the balloon blotted out any thoughts about Anya and her family, and all I could think of was how terrified I was going to be to go up, and how good it was going to feel when it was over.

For the next ten minutes or so, we watched from a distance while five guys in red coveralls hovered around the balloon as the hot air filled it. They were supervised by a white guy in a tan uniform. The sun came up quickly, the sky getting lighter and lighter as the balloon became larger and larger, still lying on its side. The bottom of the balloon was attached to a huge rectangular wicker basket that was also lying sideways, the open side facing us. It was divided into six compartments, like a set of wicker mail cubbyholes, three up and three down.

Finally, the guy in the uniform came toward the waiting passengers. When he got up close to us, Lucas poked me and whispered, "Hey, that's the guy who was in the parking lot with Prosper!"

"You're right," I said, although the big head of Mike Myers hair was hidden by a hat. "So this is Maria's boyfriend, Reggie."

"What do you think he was talking about with Prosper in the parking lot night before last?" Lucas whispered. "Maybe he and Maria are both in on the smuggling!"

"I'm not sure it means anything," I answered softly. "It could be that Prosper had just gone out to get something he'd accidentally left in the Land Rover at the same time Reggie was driving in to pick up Maria, and the two of them stopped to say hello."

"*Maybe*. Or maybe not."

He was close enough now that I didn't want to say anything more, but I thought Lucas and I could talk about it later.

Besides his tan uniform, Reggie wore dark glasses and a hat something like Prosper's, although it was tan felt instead of dark brown leather. One side of the brim was actually pinned to the crown with some kind of a medal or something.

When he had everyone's attention, he clasped his hands in front of him and said, "Ladies and gentlemen, welcome to Balloon Safaris on this lovely morning. My name is Reginald—you may call me Reggie—and I'll be your captain today." He sounded very English. I wondered if he was maybe from one of those families that had come to Kenya from Britain when it was a British colony.

"I do apologize personally for the early hour at which you had to rise this morning. You all look especially well despite the brutality of having to awaken so long before dawn."

This little speech could have sounded very stiff, but he said it with a smile, and I noticed that now all the people around me were smiling. He definitely wasn't as good looking as Uncle Geoff, but he seemed to be pretty charming.

"I would ask you to raise your hand if this will be your first hot air balloon ride."

There were seventeen of us, and all of us raised our hands except one tall guy wearing reflective sunglasses and a baseball cap.

"Right," he said. "That proportion is about normal. Gentlemen, I do not wish to humiliate you in front of your female partners, so I'm not going to ask how many of you are frightened. I expect many of you are. But on a lovely morning like this, I can guarantee you safety."

That made me feel a little bit better. And the next thing he said sounded like it was meant just for me.

"As for those of you who may have a fear of heights, let me reassure you. I have had many acrophobic passengers, and I can truly say that the vast majority of them have found the flight far more comfortable than they had expected. I have never suffered from this kind of fear myself, but I understand from what these passengers have told me that they are comforted when we are aloft by the height of the walls of the gondola, which is what we call the wicker basket behind me. If you please, step this way and I will show you how we will be traveling."

The wicker walls that divided the big rectangle of the gondola went about up to our chests. The idea, according to Reggie, was that there would be three passengers per compartment, to spread the weight around. The way it ended up was that, because we were the only kids along that day, Lucas and I were the lightest ones, so he split us up. Lucas would be in the front left compartment, and I'd be in the back left compartment. We could still stand next to each other and talk. We'd just have a wicker wall between us.

While we were all getting positioned to go, I kept looking at Reggie, wondering if he could be in on the smuggling. Finally I decided that there was no way I was going to find out just by looking at him, and for the third time so far on the trip I thought about Mom's advice to stay in my day. Whether I was going to be terrified or think it was beautiful, I didn't know for sure. But however it went, that's what I was going to concentrate on, and I would worry about the smuggling later.

One of the two other people in my compartment was a German who took pictures constantly and who didn't seem to speak any English. He was a big guy, both tall and big around. The other person was the guy with the sunglasses and the bill cap who was the only one of the passengers who'd been on a balloon ride before. While we were waiting to get up in the air, he said his name was Rolph and he was a bush pilot who flew tourists around Kenya and Tanzania. He was from Australia, but now he lived in some town not too far from where we were.

As soon as all the passengers were in, the balloon got more inflated. Reggie reached up to the burner, which was attached to a little platform over our heads, and suddenly, with a whoosh, a huge flame shot into the balloon. Seconds later we were off the ground.

"Now that we're under way," Reggie said, "I would ask you to forget your fears and simply relax and enjoy the brilliant sky and the beautiful plains of Kenya beneath us."

Unfortunately, I couldn't relax, at least not at first. In not much more than a second or two we rose as high as the top of a two-story house. I wasn't scared yet. Would I be when we got higher? I waited again.

It wasn't long before we were far enough in the air to see the shadow of the balloon on the ground in front of us racing over grass, rocks, and acacia trees.

By the time we were that far up, I knew that Reggie was right. The high wicker walls of the basket, which came almost to my shoulders, kept me from feeling like I could fall out. It was actually the fear of falling, not the fear of the height itself, that made me scared—I already knew that, kind of, from riding in airplanes. If I couldn't fall, I wasn't scared. I took a big breath of relief.

When I was finally relaxed enough to look around, I realized that the view from up there was really awesome. It wasn't very long past dawn, the sky was a solid bright orange, and the whole landscape looked golden in the morning light. It was sweet to feel the cool air and see the long, long shadows of the acacia trees on the light green grass. The hills in the distance looked purple. Streams were like pale gray ribbons, and some of the ponds reflected the blue of the sky.

Lucas, beside me, had been busy taking pictures. When she finally let her camera down, she said, "It's so quiet!"

I nodded. "It reminds me of when I go sailing with Dad, when the sails are up and the motor's off."

At first we didn't see many animals, but as the sun got higher they started to appear: a line of giraffes, then five elephants drinking from a pool. Finally we sailed over a hill and suddenly we were above an enormous herd of wildebeest and zebra. They covered the entire valley below us. Thousands and thousands and thousands of them.

"I can't believe how totally sweet this is, with all the animals getting up in the morning and moving around."

"I love the way the zebra stripes look from the air," Lucas said. "When the zebras move around inside their herd, the pattern keeps changing. Too bad we don't have a video camera."

When we moved over the next hill, either our shadow or the balloon itself seemed to scare a group of gazelles, who scampered off at top speed.

"Isn't it beautiful? This is why I love living in Africa." It was Rolph, the Australian pilot, who was standing right next to me. This was the first thing I'd heard him say since we'd introduced ourselves when we got in.

"You're right. It *is* beautiful!" I said, and meant it. "You're really lucky to live here. We've only been here a few days, and I already know that I want to come back."

"You should," he said. "I always tell my passengers that the very best thing you can do for Africa is to come back, and urge your friends to come. That helps support the tourist industry, which is very important here. Just your trip alone will put money into the hands of probably hundreds of people, and help support their families."

That brought me back to thinking about Bernard and Anya, which, I'm a little ashamed to admit, I'd pretty much forgotten, with all the scenery around us and everything.

Reggie, in the middle back compartment, kept reaching up to a valve that he used to turn the flame on for a while, then off, to make sure the air in the balloon stayed exactly hot enough to keep us up. He didn't say a lot, but every so often he'd tell us the name of a river or a hill as we flew over it, and he answered questions about the land and the animals when people asked them.

Someone asked Reggie if the balloon always took the same route.

"No," he answered. "We have to go the way the wind blows, obviously, and the wind varies. Normally the variations are not dramatic. I must say that the wind is quite uncharacteristic today. Ordinarily we stay somewhat to the west of this." Was it my imagination, or did his voice sound a little tense?

I turned toward Lucas, who was looking at something through her camera. I nudged her, and she straightened. "Lucas, did you think Reggie sounded nervous just now?"

"What? I wasn't really listening. What did he say?"

"He said the wind was taking us farther to the east than usual."

She thought a minute. "Maybe he's worried about the crew chasing us. Maybe he's wondering if the balloon will land in a place they can't get to or something."

"Oh, that's probably it," I said. If the biggest problem was waiting for the crew to find out where we were, that was a whole lot better than what I thought it might mean: that he was afraid we were going to fall out of the sky or something.

We'd floated along probably five more minutes when Reggie said, "Look, everyone, you won't want to miss this." He pointed at a natural pool up ahead and on the right. "Those in the back compartments, move forwards and as far right as possible so you can see this. The enormous black lumps in the water are hippos, having their morning bath. They'll make a great picture, so get your cameras ready."

I turned to move, like he said we should, but Lucas grabbed me by the arm and muttered, "Stay here on the left, use your binoculars, and look down over the side."

"What—" I started to say.

"Just do it," she said in a fierce whisper, and the next second she was at the front of her compartment clicking pictures of the hippos.

I got pretty meeped at this until I remembered that I'd be able to see the hippos from the back of the gondola after we'd flown over them. Anyway, I did what she asked me to do because I knew she must have a good reason.

Not many seconds later, I saw what the reason was.

Down below and off to the left, the slope of a hill rose up and up, then suddenly dropped off. Just as we passed over the highest part, someone in red came partly out of the side of the bluff below. He must have seen the shadow of the balloon passing over because he disappeared without even looking up, but not before I had a chance to see him through the binoculars. It was Jamison's son Takeshi.

I was still looking down at the opening in the hillside when I heard Lucas say, "Look, Kari, one of the hippos is sticking its head up and spouting water!" I glanced up and saw that she was talking to the place I would have been if I'd been looking at the hippos and not down at Takeshi.

"As you may know," Reggie said, "the hippopotamus is a semiaquatic animal. It has to stay in the water most of the day to maintain hydration. The hippo's calves are actually born in the water."

Rolph and the German guy were standing at the front right corner of my compartment, completely blocking Reggie's view of me. I scooted over next to them and had a chance to get a glimpse of the pool with the hippos before it passed below the balloon. I went to the back of the gondola and got a really good look at it from there.

Lucas acted like absolutely nothing had happened. When the two of us were side by side again, she took pictures and chatted to me about the group of zebras running away from us.

When the burner started up again, I whispered, "Guess what I saw!"

She totally ignored me, pointed downward, and talked about the elephants plodding along below.

It wasn't until the second time the burner came on that she looked at me and waited. I turned to face her and, in a voice just loud enough for her to hear, said, "Takeshi came out of an opening in the hillside."

It took her a split second to register the name, then her eyes got huge. "Another way into the cave!"

I nodded. I'd already figured that out.

"So *that* was what Reggie was trying to hide!"

"What are you talking about?"

"Tell you at breakfast," she said as Reggie turned off the burner.

28

The Coolest Breakfast Ever, and Beware the Shiny Object

Eventually Reggie had the burner on less and less often, and we gradually drifted downward. I couldn't believe it when we landed—it was so perfect, the gondola barely bumped as it touched the ground.

As promised, breakfast was waiting for us. Under an acacia tree stood a long table with platters of multicolored fruit and baskets of fresh breads and muffins. A man in a chef's hat was making something delicious-smelling over a portable stove.

The servers, in white uniforms and white turbans—and yes, Jeremiah was one of them—set the table with real china and silverware and took our breakfast orders. Another guy was passing out goblets half filled with orange juice, topped off with champagne for the adults.

We glanced over to where Reggie stood. He was talking to someone, but he was close enough to overhear us.

I turned back to Lucas and said, my voice louder than usual, "This whole breakfast business is like a scene out of the 1930s when rich people went on safari and took teams of servants with them. At dinner in the evening they'd actually dress up in formal clothes."

I'd learned this in one of the books I'd read before we left. I was trying to sound like we were having a completely casual conversation until we were sure nobody could hear us.

Lucas picked up my cue. "You mean like gowns and tuxedos and things?" Reggie now had his back to us and was talking to the Argentineans.

I pulled Lucas a few steps away from the rest of the guests and asked, "What's the deal with Reggie that you were going to tell me about?"

But just then, wouldn't you know, Reggie turned and announced, "Ladies and gentlemen, I've had a signal from our chef. Breakfast is served. Please be seated."

Lucas and I made sure we were sitting as far away from Reggie as possible.

There was a lot of chatter as the plates of eggs and bacon and sausages were put down and the fruit and muffins and things were passed. For a while, everybody was pretty quiet, including us, just digging into their delicious food.

As the minutes passed, the voices of the people around the table got louder.

Sometimes when I visit my dad for more than a

week or so, he'll have a party where everybody drinks
too much. So I knew that the people who were drinking
champagne and orange juice were getting a little drunk,
which probably wasn't a surprise, since it was first thing
in the morning and the waiters were pouring more champagne and orange juice every time the level in someone's
goblet got down more than an inch.

The German guy from my compartment was sitting
across the table from me next to a couple, and they were
gabbing away in German. Lucas had the last place at the
table, but I had people on my right. When things finally
got so noisy that I was sure nobody would overhear us if
we kept our voices soft, I turned and asked, "What do
you think was up with . . . him?" I jerked my head toward
Reggie.

Lucas swallowed her bite of sausage, then, in a voice
as low as mine, answered, "*Beware the shiny object.* It's
one of the Wise Attorney Tips Allen the Meep is always
giving me. He says"—she made her voice sound like a
man's—"'Lucas, when you're talking to a potential witness, be aware of misdirection. Like a magician, a witness
may wave something shiny around with his right hand to
distract you from what he's doing with his left.'"

"Excuse me, earth to Lucas. What do magicians
and shiny objects have to do with"—I took a quick look
around to make sure no one was paying attention to us—
"what's going on?"

Lucas sighed. Once in a while she gets impatient with

me because my brain is not as lightning-swift as hers.

"Dad meant that when witnesses start going into big long stories or descriptions about things that don't have anything to do with the point of what the attorney has been asking, he starts to be suspicious, because the witness may be trying to distract attention from what's really important."

"What you're saying is that you got suspicious when suddenly he started talking on and on about the hippos after he'd hardy said anything else on the whole trip?"

Lucas nodded. "And he told everybody to go up front, even though the people in the three back compartments, like you, could have seen the hippos better by looking behind the gondola after we'd flown over them. He was waving around the shiny object. He didn't want us looking down where he knew the cave was. I bet he knew Jamison's son would be down there today."

I took another bite of muffin and chewed, looking off into space while I thought about all this.

"We see Reggie talking to Prosper in the parking lot. Now it looks like Reggie has a link to Jamison's family."

Lucas nodded. "And Reggie also has a link with one of the archaeologists, don't forget."

Maria again. Somehow, obnoxious as she was, I absolutely couldn't believe she was in on the smuggling.

But Maria or no Maria, by this time we were pretty sure that Reggie *was* part of the smuggling ring, and we'd found the second entrance to the cave. I was feeling pretty good about where we were, clue-wise. If we could just tell our story to this Inspector Raza guy the professor kept talking about, the police would have to let Bernard go. Wouldn't they?

Then I had a nagging thought. "There's just this one little problem. How are we going find the cave entrance again?"

"I took a lot of pictures," Lucas answered, but her voice didn't sound all that enthusiastic.

It was obvious that she was thinking the same thing I was thinking: that the Masai Mara was a pretty big place, and a hippo pool in one part of it might look a lot like a hippo pool somewhere else. We might be totally meeped.

29

The Terrible, Horrible, No Good, Very Bad Reputation of Hippos

Jeremiah drove the Argentinean couple and Lucas and me to a game lodge, not ours, where we all got certificates saying that we had completed the balloon ride. I thought it was a little hokey, but I was also kind of proud of mine. Proud because I'd done it in spite of my fear of heights, but also because it was a super souvenir of our trip to Africa.

I had assumed all along that we'd go back to the camp in Jeremiah's van. But as it turned out, the safari drivers for the balloon guests were supposed to be waiting for us. When all the other guests were finding their drivers and heading off to their vans or Land Rovers, Jeremiah came up to us and said he'd drive us back to the camp because Bernard was in jail. For the first time that morning, he looked sad. Obviously he hadn't heard the news until after he dropped us off earlier.

"What happened to Bernard is really terrible, isn't it?" I said, getting into the van.

Jeremiah didn't say anything until he'd slid the passenger door closed and gotten into the driver's seat.

"Yes, it is very bad," he said, and that was the end of his comments. On the way out to the balloon site that morning, he'd been all friendly and perky. Now he was quiet. There were worry lines between his eyebrows, and I wondered if he and Bernard or maybe Sam were good friends.

Finally Jeremiah seemed to remember that he was working for the balloon safari company and should be friendly to the tourists, and he asked us about our experience that morning. We talked about how cool the ride was and complimented him and the cook and other servers on the delicious breakfast.

It was a little remark he made that gave us the idea we needed to find the cave's second entrance again. I happened to mention that I'd been in the same section as Rolph, and he said, "I suppose he enjoys having time to look at the animals and so on, which he probably never has time for when he is flying an aircraft. Certainly as a pilot he would know every feature of the landscape as well as any of us who work for the balloon company, including Mr. Reginald."

Lucas and I looked at each other. That's who would be able to find the hippo pool!

"You don't happen to know what company Rolph flies for?"

"Yes. He flies for a company called Safari Skies," he said, looking at us in his rearview mirror.

"I'd love to have a ride in his airplane," Lucas said. "I wonder how much it would cost."

"Maybe you could arrange something," Jeremiah said, his eyes back on the road. "I am sure someone at the lodge would be glad to call and ask on your behalf."

I looked at Lucas and mouthed the word, "Sam."

We'd been scheduled to go on a game drive with Bernard that morning after the balloon ride, but because of everything that had happened, I figured we'd be stuck at the lodge. Which wasn't all bad, I thought as we drove along. However awesome the animals were, I probably wouldn't be able to stop thinking about everything we'd found out.

Not many minutes after I'd been thinking that, something happened that got me out of those thoughts. It had to do, again, with hippos. We were going over a little bridge when we saw some of them in the water below us, and one hippo standing on the bank. Of course we'd seen them earlier from the air, but this was our first close-up view. Jeremiah stopped the van in the middle of the bridge so we could have a look. The ones in the water seemed to decide to go under just about the time we got there. They lowered themselves slowly, their enormous bodies going down first, leaving their ears, their eyes, which stuck up out of their heads, and their nostrils like slits just above the water.

"Look at that!" Lucas said. "When they go down, the last things to disappear are their eyeballs!"

"Yes," Jeremiah said, "their eyeballs are like periscopes on submarines. They allow the animals to see the world around them even when their bodies are totally submerged."

Jeremiah's van didn't have a top that would rise up, which was probably just as well, because without warning, the hippo on the bank threw himself into the pool, landing on his stomach and sending water and mud flying everywhere. A few drops even came through the crack at the top of Jeremiah's window.

"Wow, what a belly flop!" I said.

"Something must have startled him," Jeremiah said. "That is typical behavior when they are startled. Keep watching them. You may see something interesting."

Sure enough, it wasn't long before the one that had done the belly flop stuck his nostrils just above the surface and blew water out in a spout that went probably five feet into the air.

"They put on an amusing show, but in fact they are very dangerous," Jeremiah said. "They completely foul the lakes and ponds where they spend their time. People think the most dangerous animals in this part of Africa are the lions or the leopards. But except for the mosquito, which spreads malaria, the hippopotamus is the most dangerous animal of all. They kill many more people than the big cats."

"I read that they're vicious," Lucas said.

"That is true. They will attack anything that gets between them and their water source or their calves. They are easily irritated and aggressive, and people do not frighten them at all. In the ponds, they overturn boats for no reason, and they use their huge jaws and sharp teeth to tear the people into pieces. Everyone who lives around them hates them. *I* hate them."

"They look so funny!" I said. From where we were, I could see the long, oddly shaped face of one sticking out of the water.

"They do. But there is nothing funny about hippos."

Before long, we were going to find this out for ourselves.

30

A Big Day for Sam

Back at the safari camp, Jeremiah walked us to the lodge building, where we said good-bye and Lucas gave him a tip—a big one, because of his extra trouble in driving us back.

As we walked down the path to our tent, I said, "Let's make a list of all our clues and deductions to show to the professor and that inspector guy when he comes—"

"Miss Kari, Miss Lucas, I need to speak with you."

We turned around and saw Sam rushing down the path toward us. I noticed the expression on his face before he even got close. It was odd, as if he was excited, only trying not to seem excited.

"I am so glad to see you," he said when he caught us. "The professor has spoken with the park rangers and the people here at the camp, and with Bernard now in jail, I am to be your driver today. At least, I can do it for a few hours. I must be back by two o'clock this afternoon to get ready for new visitors at the lodge. I am not yet an official safari guide, but during the time I have I will do my best to show you what we will see of the beautiful Masai Mara."

So that explained it. One part of him was concerned and sad about what had happened to Anya's father, and the other part of him was totally pumped about his very first drive as a safari guide.

"That's good that you have that opportunity," I said.

"Even if it is for a rotten reason," Lucas put in.

His eyes became completely serious. "You are right. The situation with Bernard is not good. I sat with Anya late into the night, and she cried most of the time. She is a strong person, but she loves her father very much. I will tell you more when we are in the van."

"We have things to tell you, too," Lucas said.

"Come to the lodge building when you are ready to go," Sam said. Again, the corners of his mouth turned up, and I could tell there was a real smile trying to get out.

I didn't blame him for smiling in spite of what had happened to Bernard. It was a big day for Sam.

Sam pulled Bernard's van out of the driveway as if he'd spent the last ten years as a driver. When he was on the road I said, "I want to find out more about Anya and her family. Where is she now?"

"I drove her to her auntie's home in Narok this morning. Her mother was coming out from Nairobi today, so they will be together."

"Now they both have to miss work, and that's probably pretty bad for the family, too," Lucas said.

She didn't mention money, but Sam must have known what she meant, because he said, "It is not as difficult as you would think. When the professor found out what had happened, he said he would continue to pay Bernard his salary until he was found to be not guilty.

"He believes Bernard is innocent. He is in Narok waiting for his inspector friend to fly in from Mombasa. They will be here late this afternoon."

"That's wonderful news!" Lucas said, and the two of us looked at each other and smiled. We would be ready with our list of clues and deductions when he got there.

"What was it you wanted to tell me about?" Sam asked.

"There's tons of stuff," I said. "The most important thing is that when we were on the balloon ride we think we saw the second entrance to the Simba Hill cave. Or, at least, *I* saw it."

Sam's eyes got big. "That is very important! Where is it?"

"That's the problem," Lucas said. "We'd never be able to find it again on our own. But there was a pilot who flew with us and we think he might be able to go right to it since he knows the landscape so well. His name is Rolph."

"He works for Safari Skies," I added. "Do you know him?"

"I know who he is. Once or twice he has come to eat in our dining room."

"We are thinking of hiring him to fly us along the route we took so we can find the entrance again," Lucas said.

I looked at her, surprised. When she'd told Jeremiah that she might want to hire Rolph's plane, I hadn't thought she was serious. I thought it was just a cover-up for why we really wanted to contact him.

"Or maybe the professor could hire Rolph to *drive* him there," I said. I didn't think it would do any good for us to see the entrance again from an airplane. We'd be in the same pickle we were in now.

"Would you like me to call this pilot?" Sam asked. "I could say we had guests who were on the balloon safari who want to go back and explore something they saw along the way. I could ask if he thought he could retrace the route you took and see if he would be available."

I nodded. "We were hoping you'd call him. Tell him that the thing your guests want to explore is close to the hippo pool we saw. He'll know what you mean."

"I will call him when we stop for lunch and let you know what he says. Now, what were the other things you wanted to tell me?" he asked.

"First, we know who Prosper was talking to in the parking lot last night," Lucas said. "It was Reggie, the balloon pilot. And we think the two of them are working together with Jamison on the smuggling."

Sam raised his head, like an animal might if it smelled something new in the air.

"Tell him what you saw, Kari." Lucas turned to me.

I told him about Reggie sounding worried about the balloon being off its usual route, and how he tried to get everyone to look at the hippo pool. "We think he knew where that secret entrance was, and he was worried we might see exactly what I *did* see," I finished.

Sam slowed the van and took a turn to the left. "That explains several things I have seen lately," he said, shifting as the van picked up speed. "Reggie comes often to be with Maria. This has been going on for many months. It began not long after the archaeologists first came to the dig.

"In the first month or two when he was coming here, I never saw him together with Prosper. Then things changed. Perhaps five or six times in the past several weeks I have seen them talking together in the parking lot. I wondered then what they would have to talk about, but as I told you, Prosper sometimes does small jobs for people, and I thought perhaps he was doing some work for Reggie. Now, with what you are saying . . ." He shrugged. "Well, perhaps it was more than that."

"Did *you* find out anything for *us*?" Lucas asked at last.

"Oh, yes. Sorry. Well, first, about the door behind Jamison's hut. Koyati knew nothing about this, but he said he knew that Prosper used the main entrance when he brought the gift items from other villages."

Lucas and I looked at each other. So, just as we'd thought, there wasn't any good reason for him to also drive through the secret gate.

"And another interesting thing. One of the other staff members here at the lodge told me that many months ago, perhaps even a year ago, Prosper mentioned to him that when he went to school to learn to be a safari guide, Reggie was also in his class. Now, after what you told me, I am wondering if Jamison was at the same school. I know he got his education in Nairobi."

"Wow!" I said. "That could be a pretty important connection. Lucas, we're going to have to add that to our list of clues."

We ate our lunches in a place that had picnic tables, outdoor toilet facilities, and a guard on duty with a rifle or shotgun or whatever it was. Sam tried to call Rolph at Safari Skies, but it turned out to be Rolph's day off, which we probably could have figured out for ourselves if we'd thought about when he might have time to go up in a balloon. But they gave Sam Rolph's cell phone number. Unfortunately, there was no answer.

Sam put his phone back in his pocket. "If this is confidential, I thought it might not be a good idea to leave a message. I will keep trying and reach him sooner or later."

Sam had pointed out the animals as we drove—he was almost as good at spotting them as Bernard was—but we hadn't paid our usual attention because of everything we had to talk about. We were on our way back to the lodge when Sam brought the van to a stop, raised the roof, and slowly backed up. "I saw something you will want to see, and I do not want to frighten it."

He put on the brakes and pointed into the branches of a tree close to the road. "Look up there," he said softly.

I had to go over to the side where Lucas was sitting. At first, all I saw when I looked up at the tree was leaves. Then slowly the animal's silhouette came into focus, and finally I could see the spots. "A leopard!" I whispered.

"Oh, there it is," Lucas said, also with a hushed voice. "What's dangling underneath?"

"It's prey," Sam said. "I think it is an impala."

I saw it then: the silhouette of an antelope hanging upside down under the leopard.

"How did he get it up there?" Lucas asked.

"Yeah, the impala is almost as big as he is!" I added.

"Leopards are very powerful animals."

"I feel sorry for him . . . or her. The impala I mean," I said.

"You could say that humans do worse things," Sam said. "We raise millions of animals just to kill them for food. At least the impala lived a life of freedom."

❖   ❖   ❖

When we were back on the road, I said, "Four out of the Big Five! Or five, if you count that lion." We explained to him what Bernard had said about waiting until we saw one close up.

"It is unusual you have not had a closer view yet," Sam said. "Lions are plentiful in the Masai Mara. I am sure you will see one very soon."

"Yeah, promises, promises," Lucas joked.

Sam smiled in the rearview mirror. We were all so lighthearted about what it might mean to see a lion.

31

The Sound That Might Have Been a Baboon

We got back to the lodge in time for Sam to be at work by two. Lucas and I were going to write up our list of clues. We talked about it as we walked down the path, deciding to do a rough draft of it in the tent, then go up to the lodge and use a computer to type it. Then we could make copies of our list for Uncle Geoff, the professor, and his inspector friend. Having all the clues and deductions on paper would be better than trying to explain everything. Although, knowing adults, I figured we'd probably have to explain everything anyway.

As soon as we got back in the tent, I pulled out my journal and lay on my stomach. Lucas kicked off her sandals and lay on her back, her hands under her head.

We were both quiet for a while, trying to figure out what to put down first. I fiddled with my automatic pencil for a while, then said, "One of the things Mom is always saying is that the most important part of a writing job can be figuring out how to organize everything. She says you have to think really hard about what she calls *organizing your material for maximum effectiveness*. I think we should figure out how to do that with all our clues and deductions."

Lucas pulled herself off the bed and went from window to window, zipping all of them shut. "We should probably be careful and keep our voices down. Remember how easy it was for us to overhear Maria the other night."

I made a guilty face. "I should have thought of that."

"It's okay," she said, "there's nobody out here and I think almost everybody is gone from the whole camp except the staff. But we should probably stay on the safe side."

She finished the last of the windows and flopped back down. "Now, where were we?"

"Organizing our material," I said.

We were both quiet for a while.

"We need a title," I said.

Another silence. "How about *The Simba Hill Criminal Network*?" Lucas offered.

"How about *The Simba Hill Criminal Conspiracy*?"

"Yeah, that's better," she said.

"Should we start from the beginning and go to the end?" I asked. "I mean, what happened first, what happened next—like that?"

We talked about it for a while. In the end, we decided to do a summary at the beginning, saying that we believed Jamison and his family, Prosper, and Reggie had worked together to dig up and smuggle out the artifacts. That went on one page. After that we had three pages, each with a title on it: *The Case against Jamison*, *The Case against Prosper*, and *The Case against Reggie*.

"Okay, first Jamison," I said.

We started in, me writing as fast as I could as we went over the clues. I wrote about the space at the back of Jamison's house, the gate, the door, the tire tracks that matched Prosper's vehicle, Prosper collecting the gift shop things from other villages but delivering them through the main entrance, what had happened on the balloon ride, and the meetings between Prosper and Reggie. Some of the things, like that one, were clues about two people, so I had to write them twice.

"Prosper and Reggie were classmates in safari school," Lucas said.

I raised my pencil to write that on the Prosper page first.

That's when I heard the rustling. I sucked in my breath and looked toward the side of the tent where the noise had come from.

It was obvious from Lucas's expression that she hadn't heard it. But she *had* heard my little gasp. Her eyes and eyebrows had an expression that asked what was up.

I mouthed, "Keep talking," and crept silently to the window nearest where the sound had come from. I swallowed. My mouth was suddenly dry.

"You also have to write that on the Reggie page," she said. "Oops, I think I'm going to sneeze. I need a Kleenex."

She got up, pointed at the bathroom, and mouthed, "Window."

The ventilation window above our toilet stool looked out at the shrubbery. Biting my lip, I gave her time to stand up on the toilet seat. My heart was thudding now in a way that almost hurt.

One, two, three, I said to myself, and pulled the window zipper open with a quick gesture.

A branch cracked in the shrubbery. I listened for more sounds, but all I could hear was the pumping of blood in my ears.

Lucas reappeared in the doorway.

"Did you see something?" I asked.

"Just a little movement in the shrubbery. It might have been a dik-dik," she said, sounding uncertain.

I shook my head. "Whatever I heard, it was way bigger than a dik-dik. Didn't you hear that branch crack?"

"It might have been a baboon. Remember? Bernard said they've been having problems with baboons getting into the complex."

I must have looked as skeptical as I was feeling,

because Lucas said, "I don't think it could've been a person, Kari. I mean, except for the staff, we're practically the only people around here this afternoon. Unless our list of deductions is completely wrong and there's somebody on the staff working with Reggie and Prosper and Jamison's family. But who could it be? Prosper's driving the professor around, and I can't imagine that Reggie or Jamison or one of his sons snuck into the compound and somehow found our tent just in case we made a list of clues they could overhear."

"I guess you're right. I don't know why I'm so spooked. Ever since we got here I feel like my intuition has been just a little off. It must have been a baboon."

I bit my lip again, and added, "We'd better hope it was a baboon."

32

Intuition for Sure

If we'd been overheard, then the damage was done. But just to be on the safe side, we headed to the lodge and sat in a lonely corner of the lobby and finished our list in whispers. I was in the middle of reading the final handwritten version to Lucas when Sam came out of one of the office doors and headed in our direction, a big smile on his face.

"The professor called. He said he and the inspector should arrive here at the camp at about four thirty."

I looked at my watch. A little less than an hour to go.

"And here is the truly good news," he said, his eyes shining, "Anya and Bernard will be with them. Bernard is now out on bail!"

Lucas and I looked at each other and smiled. "That totally rocks!" I said.

"Oh, and in all the excitement I almost forgot to tell

you something important," Sam said. "I finally reached the pilot, Rolph. He is fully booked over the next several days. But he said you did not really need *him*. What you needed was a map." He reached into a pocket of his green uniform pants and held up a piece of paper. "He faxed it. And by the way, I made sure I was the only one at the fax machine when it came through."

Rolph hadn't drawn the map himself. Instead he'd used part of a large, printed map of the Masai Mara and marked it up. There was a line with the words BALLOON ROUTE written next to it. The best part was the two cute little hippos he'd drawn under the word POOL.

The roads on the map didn't seem to have any numbers or anything. "Sam, do you think somebody like Bernard would know how to find the hippo pool from looking at this?" I asked.

"Oh yes. Easily. It is a drive of about forty-five minutes from here, but the pool would not be difficult to find. I believe *I* could even find it. And that broken line just beside the pool," he said, pointing it out, "means there is a dirt track leading to it. Land Rovers are better for off-road use, but even a van could travel that route."

Lucas, her eyes still on the map, said, "Sweet!"

It took us nearly a half hour to get our Simba Hill Criminal Conspiracy lists typed up. By the time we'd printed them out, made copies of the lists and map, and put them in envelopes for Uncle Geoff, Professor Wanjohi, and Inspector Raza, it was twenty past four.

With all that finished, Lucas was ready to head for the door. "You want to go outside and wander around until they get here?" she asked.

I shook my head.

"What do you want to do, then?"

"I want to stay here."

Lucas pulled her eyebrows together. "Why?"

I shrugged. "I feel safe here with people around. There's something about this whole thing that feels . . . dangerous. I want those guys arrested."

She shrugged. "Okay, if you say so." In spite of what happened at the tent, Lucas is usually pretty respectful about my intuition. "What are you going to do?"

"I thought I'd send an e-mail to Mom telling her what's been going on and attach our list of clues. You could help me figure out what to say. It would give us something to do."

"Okaaaay." The drawn-out word sounded skeptical, but at least she was going along with my plan.

A few seconds of silence passed while we pulled up our chairs at the computer again.

"Do you think the professor and his friend will . . ." I said, letting the sentence trail off while I looked for the right words.

"Take us seriously?" Lucas supplied.

I nodded.

"I think they will if we can show them the second entrance to the cave."

"Maybe we should show the list to Uncle Geoff first. He knows we've already solved two mysteries so we know about clues and things. Maybe he could, like, speak up for us."

"Good idea."

"I hope we can get it cleared up right away. I want those guys arrested."

"You already said that," Lucas said.

"I know. But I can't stop thinking about it."

33

Telling Our Story

At four thirty-five we heard voices coming up the path from the parking lot. Not just the professor and his inspector friend, but the whole Simba Hill crowd had arrived.

It was like a parade of smiling people. First came Bernard and Anya, with Sam at her side, all of them with huge smiles on their faces. Behind them was Professor Wanjohi, totally beaming. The other archaeologists came next, and even Maria was smiling, which surprised me a little. With them was a man in a tan uniform—I'd expected him to have a gun in a holster, but he didn't—who seemed to be smiling just because everybody else was.

Lucas and I ran over to Bernard and Anya to give them hugs. It was *so* good to see them. Except for us and the two women behind the reception desk, the lobby had been pretty much empty and quiet since we'd gotten there. Now it was filling up, with people coming through every door. Everyone was happy and laughing.

Professor Wanjohi was now standing near Lucas and me. "It's a very good day for Bernard and his family," he said with a grin.

It seemed to me it would be a much better day once there were *no* charges against Bernard, but I didn't say anything about that.

The professor turned to his friend. "Lucas and Kari, I would like you to meet Inspector Raza Jahagirdar. Raza, this is Geoff's niece, Kari, and her friend Lucas. I'm sorry," he said to us, "I don't remember your last names."

"And speaking of last names," the inspector said, "I do not expect you to remember mine. It is very difficult for people outside my culture. You may just call me Raza, as Professor Wanjohi does."

Raza looked like he might be from India or Pakistan, and his name, whatever it had been—I'd already forgotten it—had sounded that way, too. I remembered Lucas telling me in one of her mini-lectures that Mombasa had a large Indian and Pakistani population.

Raza and the two of us said a few polite things to each other. But it wasn't long before his attention turned back to Bernard and Anya.

Uncle Geoff turned to go, and Lucas and I followed him out of the building. "Uncle Geoff, could you stop at our tent? There's something we want to talk to you about."

We walked down the path together talking about how great it was to have Anya and Bernard back.

"What's up?" Uncle Geoff asked when we got inside the tent.

I handed him his envelope. "There's a list of clues in here. Actually three lists, and a map," I said. "We think we know who's been in on the smuggling. And we think we can use the map that's in there to find the second entrance to the Simba Hill cave."

Uncle Geoff dropped onto the side of one of the beds and his eyebrows went way up. "You're serious?"

I nodded, and the two of us sat down across from him. "Read it."

We waited while he read all three lists and looked at the map.

At last he looked up. "How did you two get all this information?"

"It's a long story," Lucas said. "But we have copies of the lists and map for Professor Wanjohi and the inspector. Would you mind if we saved the explanation until after we've shown it to them? Because they'll just ask us to say everything all over again."

I added, "We came to you first because you know that we've solved some mysteries in the past, so we're pretty good at clues and things."

"And you want me to go with you and tell them to take you seriously?"

"Would you?" I asked.

"I'll do what I can."

A few minutes later, we were in the professor's tent. He and Raza sat on the side of one of the beds facing Uncle Geoff, with Lucas and me on the other. Lucas was closest to the door, where she could pop up now and then to look out the entrance flap and the windows to make sure nobody was out there listening.

Uncle Geoff started out. "Kari and Lucas have gathered some information about the crime you're here to investigate, Inspector, um, Raza. And I think you might want to pay attention to them. They're quite good detectives."

He explained about how we'd solved the mystery of the forged Rembrandt painting and rescued our friend Seneca.

"Rather impressive work in both cases," he said. "And now they've come up with a list of clues, actually several lists, that they believe will tell you who is looting the Simba Hill site. They also seem to think they can take you to where the second entry to the cave is located. I've read the lists and looked at the map, and I think you should take them seriously."

That seemed to be the signal for me to hand the two guys their envelopes. Once again we sat and waited while they read through everything.

"The last piece of paper is the map showing where I

saw Jamison's son coming out of the bluff," I said.

Professor Wanjohi turned to his friend. "Raza, you met Prosper today, but you do not know the others. I know Jamison by reputation only, but Reggie is a familiar figure here. He is courting Maria."

He turned to us. "Now you must tell us how you acquired all of this information."

We spent the next half hour talking about what we'd seen and heard and showing everyone the pictures Lucas had taken. Every so often Uncle Geoff would get a worried look on his face and tell us he didn't approve of something we'd done, and a couple of times someone asked about something they hadn't really understood. But all in all it went pretty well.

When we got to the end, Inspector Raza said, "It looks as if we have many leads to examine. First, of course, we need to get to that cave entrance and block it off as a crime scene. Then we'll have to see if we can find anything incriminating in Jamison's village or Reggie's home, wherever that is. It may take some time, of course, but if what you have written here is true, you have been a great help to us."

He looked down at the map. "How far away is this second cave entrance?"

"Sam told us it was about forty-five minutes from here," Lucas said.

The professor looked at his watch. "It's a quarter

of six now. Raza, what would you think of heading out there this evening? We don't want to make a fuss and call attention to the fact that we're leaving, but perhaps we could get Anya to put together some bread and cheese and so on as a substitute for dinner and be on our way." He tapped his finger on the map. "A great deal hinges on whether this location really is the scene of the looting."

"I think that's wise," the inspector said. "If it *is* a crime scene, we can call for a team of park rangers to post an armed guard."

Less than a half hour later we were on our way to the parking lot. Lucas and I would be going in the van with my uncle, a police inspector, and the head of the African Rock Art Society. At first, Raza hadn't approved of Bernard driving the van, because he was still officially a suspect. But our list of deductions must've been pretty convincing. When the professor argued that Bernard was the only experienced driver he really trusted, Raza muttered something about strength of evidence in Bernard's favor and that was all he said about it. Bernard made a point of telling us that he would have his trusty gun under the seat to protect us from any animals once we got out of the van. It was a set-up even the Ghost of Mom would approve of, I thought.

But that's when I noticed something. "What's that police van doing there?" I asked as we neared the lot.

The professor, who was walking next to me, said, "It's on loan from the police in Narok." I must have looked puzzled, because he added, "Raza and I used it to get here this afternoon."

"From the Narok police station?" I asked.

"Yes." He sounded surprised by my question. I couldn't blame him. I must have sounded like an idiot.

"Prosper didn't drive you?"

"No. He drove me to the station, but when the police agreed to loan us the van, I gave him the rest of the day off. The other guard was on duty at Simba Hill."

I asked if he knew where Prosper had gone or what he'd done that afternoon. Of course he didn't.

But *I* knew where Prosper had gone and what he'd done. He'd come back to the lodge and listened at our tent as Lucas and I created our list of clues and deductions. There wasn't a doubt in my mind.

34

Night Drive

"Lucas, guess what," I muttered as people were getting into the van. "Prosper wasn't with the professor this afternoon. He had the afternoon off. What if he was the one who made the noise outside the tent?"

"I'm sure it was an animal, Kari." She looked around the parking lot. "Besides, Prosper's Land Rover is over there. So I don't think we're in a lot of danger from him."

I thought about that. Maybe she was right. Maybe I was overthinking everything.

That close to the equator, night comes at exactly six o'clock. And it goes from being day to night in only a few minutes—no twilight, like we get in Minnesota. So by a quarter to seven, the sunlight was completely gone.

I have to admit, it was nice to be out in the dark, away from any lights except the almost full moon, which was still big and close to the horizon, and the stars and our headlights. Away from people and sounds.

The passengers in the van stayed mostly quiet, too. Every so often, the professor would drum his fingers on the side of his car seat, like he was nervous. It seemed like he and everybody else were kind of holding their breath, waiting to see if we really would find that second entrance to the cave. I didn't have any doubt about that. If we got to the hippo pool, I could show them exactly where it was.

The moonlight shone on the trees and bushes, and when we saw ponds or drove over streams, the water glittered. Probably the most beautiful scene was a string of giraffes on top of a hillside, silhouetted against the moon. It's a sight I will remember my whole life.

Bernard said that vehicles weren't supposed to stop in the Masai Mara at night, but that didn't mean we couldn't see any animals. We saw elephants off to one side and, later, ostriches on the other. A couple of times we actually *had* to stop because there were animals in the road. First it was a group of Grant's gazelles. They stared at us in terror, their incredibly long, graceful horns pointing to the moon.

Later we stopped for a herd of cape buffalo blocking our way. The eyes of the nearest ones glowed red in our headlights. The herd didn't seem to want to go anywhere very fast, so Bernard switched off the engine and raised the top of the van, and everyone stood up and listened to them snuffle away, until there was nothing ahead but silence and moonlight.

For most of the trip we were driving on a regular gravel road. Eventually we turned right onto a rough dirt track. Really just two ruts with grass in between, like the drive to the dig site.

"We're getting very close now," Bernard said. "We should be there in less than ten minutes."

We hadn't gone far when we slowed for some deep bumps—it must have rained there in the past day or so, because the road was still a little damp, and some animals had made huge tracks.

"Hippo tracks, I believe," Bernard said. "I do not see any near us, which is a good thing. Although they are plant eaters and we are not food to them, they do not like humans, and they are very strong. If they thought we were between them and their pool they could attack us. And even two or three of them could destroy the van and everyone in it."

That thought had just gotten my heart and imagination working overtime when the track curved sharply, and suddenly we were looking at four lions. Smack in front of us. Staring at us.

My heart gave a jolt and my pulse pounded loud in my ears.

The van screeched to a stop. I heard the professor catch his breath, and Lucas said, "Omigod!"

"I am not certain what is going on here," Bernard said.

Three of the lions were male. Two had light-colored manes. The third was bigger, with a slightly darker mane.

"Whatever they're up to, I am not sure we want to be in the middle of it," Uncle Geoff said.

"That's what was I was thinking," I muttered.

"Actually, the lions cannot hurt us inside the van, but I am still a bit worried about the hippos who made those tracks," Bernard said. "I have my foot on the brake, but when the lions get out of our way, we will speed ahead."

But the lions didn't get out of our way. Eventually, they seemed to forget we were there, and in the full glare of the headlights they turned to stare at each other.

We watched as the two younger males faced off against the older, larger one. The female stood off to one side.

Bernard said, "I believe those two younger males want to fight the older one for mating rights with the lioness."

The big male was focusing on one of the two rivals. He raised his head, opened his mouth, and roared.

Even inside the van the sound was terrifying. I covered my mouth with both hands and caught my lower lip between my teeth.

One of the smaller males took the side of the other, and suddenly it was the two of them against the big guy.

Bernard's voice dropped to a whisper. "Look at the lioness."

She was out of the direct glow of the headlights, but we could see her clearly. She had fallen into a crouch.

With a great snarl she sprang at the two younger males. Moving like lightning, the two disappeared into the brush.

The big male and the lioness chased them only a short distance.

"I believe we will not wait for the romantic encounter," Bernard said as our van bumped down the track.

"That scared the meep out of me!" I said, and heaved a great breath.

"Scared the meep out of me, too," Uncle Geoff said.

"Bernard," Lucas asked, "in a fight between hippos and lions, who would win?"

"It would depend on how many lions there were. A single lion cannot kill a hippo. I have known of cases where three lions have brought a hippo down. But it is not uncommon for a mother hippo to kill a lion to defend her calf. In general, lions tend to have great respect for hippos."

We came over a hill. "I think I see our pool up ahead," Bernard said.

I was about to pull out the map Rolph had sent and try to get oriented when Bernard spoke again. "Oh dear. There are the hippos. Excuse my driving. This is going to be rough. I need to speed through this area as quickly as I can. It is not good to be between hippos and their water."

He sped to the bottom of the hill. The pool was on the left and the hippos, just visible in the moonlight, were grazing maybe the length of a football field off to our right. There were six or seven of them. It was hard to tell in the moonlight. We were so busy looking at them that none of us saw the mud until it was too late.

The puddle was huge, glimmering yards ahead in the headlights. Bernard tried to power through, but it was no use. He shifted from first gear into reverse and back again, gunning the engine. Then he did it again and again. We rocked forward and backward, gaining a few inches every time.

For a second there I thought we were going to make it. But just as it seemed the van was going to pull out of the mud at last, I caught sight of Bernard's expression in the rearview mirror. He was no longer looking directly ahead, but off to the side. He looked worried. And if Bernard was worried, I was worried.

That's when I saw the Land Rover.

It swung out from behind a nearby bush and stopped directly in front of us, facing our van. Suddenly Takeshi and Sunte appeared at our side windows, spears raised.

I gasped, and my heart pounded with sheer panic.

In their village in the daytime, the two brothers had looked interesting but not dangerous. Here at night, with their spears, they were warriors. Deadly, and absolutely terrifying.

Bernard scrambled under the passenger seat for the gun. Both Raza and Professor Wanjohi pulled their cell phones out of their pockets and stabbed in numbers.

Before the gun was out, before the calls could be made, the windows on both sides shattered. Sunte yanked the driver's door open and pulled Bernard out. With a single thrust of his spear, Takeshi knocked Raza's phone from his hand and stabbed Professor Wanjohi in the shoulder.

I screamed and grabbed Uncle Geoff's arm.

Reggie and Prosper appeared behind the Maasai. Reggie pulled the van's sliding door open. "Get out! All of you!"

My eyes and mouth were wide, and I held my breath in terror as Raza jumped out of the van and helped the injured professor. Professor Wanjohi came behind him slowly, blood oozing from his wound.

Uncle Geoff grabbed my hand and squeezed it hard. I looked from him to Lucas, my heart clutched in terror. Would tonight would be the last time I would ever see them? Were we all going to die?

35

Simba

Uncle Geoff followed Raza out of the van. Behind me, Lucas whispered one word: "Karate."

She gave me a gentle shove from behind. "We can do this," she muttered. We'd been taking karate lessons. Was there a chance we could use what we'd learned?

Prosper walked around to the driver's side of the van and reached inside, and the engine fell silent, although the headlights were still on. He put the key in his pocket.

The Maasai warriors stood in front of us, spears out, daring anyone to make a move.

Reggie stood between them. "I'm sorry it has to end like this for all of you," he said. Then, looking at Lucas and me, he added, "You have these young women to blame."

"Are you aware that my colleagues know about the three of you?" Raza asked.

"Your colleagues in Narok? I don't believe we have anything to worry about from the Narok police."

The professor had been leaning against the van, holding his injured shoulder. Out of the corner of my eye I saw him inching toward the open door. *The gun*, I thought. *He wants to get Bernard's gun.*

"You may have bought them off," Raza was saying, "but if all of us are killed, *someone* is going to have to answer for it."

"Because you are attacked by animals? I don't think so."

The professor, now very close to the open door of the van, was jerked away by Sunte. He fell to the ground, and Sunte, the total meep, kicked him. Takeshi slammed the van door shut. Raza kneeled at the professor's side.

Lucas raised her arm for a karate chop on Sunte, but before she could deliver it he had her wrist in his hand.

Reggie backed toward the Land Rover, his eyes on us.

That was when I realized that their plan was simply to leave us there. Leave us for the hippos to trample.

They didn't expect a fight.

Prosper turned to follow Reggie.

Bernard and Uncle Geoff looked at each other, then back and forth between the two of them.

The result was incredibly fast. Bernard took one step toward Prosper and kicked him right between his legs. Prosper screamed and fell to the ground. Startled,

Reggie spun around, and Uncle Geoff socked him smack in the jaw.

Reggie stumbled backward, but didn't fall. Without stopping to think, I darted out from behind Uncle Geoff and gave Reggie the hardest karate kick I could give him right in his stomach. He grabbed his middle and went down next to Prosper, who was writhing and whimpering.

Somehow everybody seemed to know that I had taken charge of guarding the two guys on the ground. Prosper was still down there, holding his crotch with both his hands. Reggie rolled over and got on his hands and knees, and now I kicked *him* between the legs.

Prosper and Reggie were easy to fight, but the warriors were another story. When I looked up, Bernard, Raza, and Uncle Geoff, backs to me, were lined up in front of Takeshi. Spear out, his face bright from the van's headlights, the Maasai looked ready to stab whoever came at him.

For a moment no one moved. It was like a still part in the middle of a dance. I wondered who would be the one to take the next step.

At last Uncle Geoff launched forward and reached to where Takeshi held the spear. But the Maasai was a trained warrior. One quick move and the spear sliced into Uncle Geoff's hand.

Bernard jumped toward Takeshi and slammed him sideways with his whole body. The Maasai struggled to keep his balance. Raza, coming from the other side, tried to wrestle Takeshi to the ground.

Uncle Geoff looked down to where he was bleeding. When he looked up again, his glance moved away from the fight in front of him and his eyes filled with horror.

I turned toward what he had seen, and gasped.

Lucas was in Sunte's grip. He held her tightly across her chest with one arm. The other held a spear pointed at her throat.

My heart jumped, then pounded in my ears. My hands went to my face. I stood there, frozen, terrified by what was in front of my eyes.

I finally found my voice. *"Lucas!"* Everyone turned to where she stood, chin high, spear tip at her throat. She and Sunte were well back in the track where the Land Rover and van faced each other. The scene was bright in the van's headlights.

I was too filled with fear to notice the lights or the noise from a third vehicle until it bumped to a stop in the grass beside Bernard's van. I swear it was still moving when Sam jumped out of the driver's seat, and Anya and Charlie appeared around the other side.

Now Sam had hold of Prosper, who was struggling to his feet. They didn't see Lucas and Sunte between the other two vehicles.

"Stop!"

The voice came from over Lucas's head. Charlie,

Sam, and Anya turned and looked to where Sunte held her, his face cruel.

"Everyone who came with Bernard, and you three, go stand by his van or I will cut this girl's throat. Do it *now*."

None of us moved. I think we were all in shock.

"MOVE! NOW!" he shouted again. And we all instantly moved toward where the professor still lay on the ground.

Reggie scrambled to his feet. Prosper limped toward the van Sam had driven.

Sunte pressed the spear tip closer to Lucas's throat. I pulled my own neck back as far as it would go, as if that would help. My heart raced with pure terror. I was sure Sunte would kill her before Reggie and Prosper made their escape.

Lucas's eyes slid to the right and suddenly they grew huge.

I looked over my shoulder, following her gaze.

The female lion, low to the ground, was moving slowly toward us.

My heart jumped again, and I tasted blood as I bit into my lip. The lion was the length of a classroom away, in a patch of long grass.

There was a whisper of a noise, and Sunte raced past me toward the lion.

This was the fight the Maasai brothers were born for.

In an instant they were between the rest of us and the animal, spears raised, waiting.

I watched, terrified, fascinated.

Three seconds passed. Four. Everything was very, very still.

Then the ground trembled and the pounding started. Hippos. Running.

The lioness raised her head, and with one graceful spring turned and was gone.

The warriors, too, looked at the charging hippos and disappeared into the brush, Sunte trailing behind Takeshi, limping.

Lucas was beside me. I reached out for her, but got Uncle Geoff instead. He grabbed the two of us—Lucas with his good hand and me with his other arm around my elbow—and pulled us behind Sam and Anya, back to the van they'd come in. Charlie and Raza lifted the professor between them.

We scrambled in with the thundering sound of hippos nearer by the second. Charlie crashed the passenger door closed as Bernard slammed the van in gear, and off we went.

I looked back.

Prosper and Reggie jumped into the Land Rover, Reggie in the driver's side. Beyond them the entire herd of giant animals ran at amazing speed across the grass, the pounding of their steps incredibly loud above the sound of the engine.

Bernard wheeled the van around in a turn so sharp and fast it sent everyone flying.

Behind us, Reggie sped the Land Rover backward, his tires spitting dust and gravel. Bernard's van, the one we'd ridden in for days, now stuck in the mud, rolled onto its side and was flattened as the hippos trampled it.

36

After the Crisis

Bernard pulled his phone out of his pocket and handed it to Raza, who was in the passenger seat up front next to him. The blood was still so loud in my ears that I barely heard the sound of Raza's voice as he spoke angrily into the phone in Swahili.

Uncle Geoff held his handkerchief against the cut in his hand. "It's not that bad," he said when he saw me looking at it. "I was lucky."

Charlie, torso now bare, had taken off his outer shirt, whipped off his undershirt, and held the soft cloth against the professor's wounded shoulder. "This isn't life threatening, but it needs to be looked at."

The inspector snapped the phone shut, handed it back to Bernard, and turned to talk to the rest of us. "We're going to Narok. Clearly I need to supervise the police activities." His voice had a definite sarcastic ring to it.

"And we will take the professor"—he looked at Uncle Geoff holding his bleeding hand—"the *two* professors to the district hospital there."

I undid my seat belt to hug Lucas again. It had been at least ten seconds since the last time I'd hugged her.

She struggled a little—I think I was practically smothering her—and said, "I can't believe the guy who held me could run like that. I broke a bone in his foot."

I fell back into my seat. "You *broke* a *bone* in his *foot*!? *How?*" I asked.

Lucas, who had everyone's attention by this time, sounded just the tiniest bit shook up. But not anything like I'd be if I were in her situation.

"I tried to give him a karate chop, but he caught my wrist. He spun me around and I jabbed him with my elbow. That's when he grabbed me and held me next to him, the way you saw. I thought of that self-defense course we took, and I stomped my foot as hard as I could on his bare instep. I actually heard a crack.

"He grunted—I couldn't believe he didn't yell louder or let go of me, because I knew I'd broken a bone. I know that the Maasai warriors learn early not to show pain, but still, it was amazing.

"Anyway, instead of letting me go, he held me tighter with the one arm, and used the other to hold his spear against my neck. I wanted to yell for help, but I was sure he'd cut my throat if I did. So I stood there and waited for somebody to notice me.

"Then, when you all were staring at us and he was telling everybody what to do, I looked over to see if the hippos were getting ready to attack, and that's when I saw the lion. He saw it, too, and pushed me aside into the hood of the Land Rover. The next second he was in the lion's face."

Except for Bernard, whose eyes were on the road, every single person in the van was staring at her. Even Raza, who was completely turned around in his seat. Maybe because I knew how brave she was, I was the only one there who wasn't completely speechless. "Weren't you terrified?"

"I was . . . a *little* scared he might kill me because I broke his foot and I was a girl."

I hadn't thought of that, but it made sense that a Maasai warrior would be humiliated being hurt by a girl. I was sure he would have killed her if it hadn't been for the lioness, but Lucas was only a *little* scared. I thought of how she might have reacted if he'd held a spider in front of her instead.

"But you're okay. He didn't hurt you," Raza said.

"No. I'm fine." When nobody moved, she added, "Really. I'm fine. You can stop staring at me."

Raza's eyes shifted to the back seat where Sam, Anya,

and Charlie were crowded together. "How did you know we would need help?"

Charlie looked at Sam, and Sam looked at Anya. "Prosper didn't come to dinner," she said, shrugging. "He had never missed dinner before. Not once. Prosper is a big man, and he likes his food.

"I asked someone I work with if he had seen Prosper, and he said, yes, he had seen him with Reggie in the parking lot. I wondered if they had somehow found out that you were leaving and knew where you were going. I thought it would not be a bad thing if some of us went to make sure you returned safely. I left the dining room and found Sam. The people at my tables are probably still waiting for me to come and refill their water glasses," she finished with a small smile.

"After Anya found me, we found Charlie," Sam said.

He turned, and Charlie took up the story. "It sounded suspicious to me. So we commandeered the first vehicle we could find with a key in it. I let Sam take the wheel because he knows how to drive on these back roads." He looked at Lucas and me and twitched his mustache. "God knows *I* don't."

"Sam is a very good driver," Anya said, looking at her fiancé with pride.

"Bernard, how did they stop your van?" Sam asked.

"They made mud in the tire tracks somehow," Bernard said. "From barrels of water, I suppose."

"It was a good thing we came." Charlie's voice sounded lighthearted, as usual.

"It would have turned out very differently if you hadn't," Lucas said, much more seriously.

Suddenly, I started to cry.

37

What Happened to the Bad Guys, Maria Gets Humble, and a New Archaeological Site

"Okay, that's out of the way," I said. I pulled off my T-shirt and flopped onto the lounge chair next to where Lucas was lying, soaking up the rays at the pool.

"Was she mad?"

"No. I guess Uncle Geoff called her last night from the hospital, so she already knew about the attack, and she knew that Charlie, Sam, and Anya had come to our rescue. But it sounded like he didn't tell her anything about the spear or the lion or the hippos."

"I suppose you told her all about those things. In great detail." Lucas didn't even open her eyes when she said this.

"Yeah. Right." Like I would *ever* tell Mom about those things. "I'm supposed to call her again in a few days when we find out what happens to everybody. Hey, that reminds me, guess who I saw leaving?"

"Who?"

"While I was up at the lodge, I saw Maria walking out with a police officer guy, and she had a suitcase."

This got Lucas to open her eyes. "A suitcase! Seriously?"

I nodded.

"Did anybody say why?"

"No. Nobody seemed to know anything more than we do."

"So maybe she *was* in on it!" Lucas's whole face lit up when she said this.

"Maybe." I shrugged. "And I saw Bernard, too. All the charges against him have been dropped."

"Duh."

"Yeah, I know. But here's something new: the Park Rangers found the second entrance to the Simba Hill cave and they have it all closed off."

"Really? Already?"

"Yeah, they did it last night, I guess. They used our map. They said the entrance was almost exactly at the spot I marked."

"Cool!"

I lay back in the chair and closed my eyes. It felt good to be lying there beside the pool, doing something that was completely normal, instead of running around being attacked by bad guys and wild animals. We still had about a week to go in our vacation. I hoped it was going to be a lot more calm than the time we'd had so far.

"That's all pretty big news. You learn anything else when you were up there?"

"No one has heard anything about Prosper and Reggie and Jamison. Oh, another thing. The professor is still in the hospital."

"That's too bad," Lucas said. She was quiet for a while, then said, "But the police took Maria away, and she had a suitcase with her."

"Yup. I saw it with my very own eyes."

"That has to mean something."

That was Friday. We didn't take any game drives the whole weekend because, of course, Bernard's van had been wrecked and we weren't all that interested in going with someone else. Bernard caught a ride into Nairobi with another safari group so he could get a different van from the company he worked for. But staying at the lodge was kind of a good thing, as it turned out, because news was coming in fast, and we got to hear it right away.

Anya told us on Saturday that she'd heard that Inspector Raza had immediately taken a team of policemen to Jamison's village to look at the space behind Jamison's hut. Somebody had cleaned out the artifacts, but they'd done it in a hurry and missed some little shards and things. So the police were able to use that evidence to arrest Jamison on suspicion of smuggling. They'd also found some evidence in Reggie's house, but Prosper, Reggie, and Jamison's sons were all still missing.

On Sunday, when we were at the pool again, Sam came to tell us that Prosper had been arrested in Nairobi. He'd been hiding out in a friend's apartment, but as soon as Saturday night came, he decided to go to a bar. Somebody recognized him from the picture that had been in the newspaper on Friday, and they called the cops.

"The newspaper picture showed him with his hat on," Sam said. "So what does he do? He wears his hat to the bar." He shook his head, like he couldn't quite believe how stupid that was.

The professor came back to the safari camp on Sunday. His arm was in a sling, but except for that he seemed okay. We'd seen him earlier in the day, but we didn't actually have a chance to talk to him until dinner.

As soon as we were done asking him how he was and everything, I asked if he'd heard if Reggie or Jamison's sons had been arrested.

"As far as I know, they haven't been found yet." He was trying to butter his toast using only one hand. That was obviously not working very well, so Charlie took the piece of toast and did it for him.

"What about Maria?" Lucas asked. "On Friday, Kari saw her leave with a suitcase."

Even with his arm in a sling, up until that point the professor had still had his usual fill-up-the-room energy. Now he turned toward us and heaved a big sigh, and when he let his breath out, his energy seemed to leave him, like air leaving a balloon. "That's a very sensitive subject, but I suppose you will all have to hear it sooner or later. One of the things the police found in Reggie's home was a journal full of information in his own handwriting on archaeological methods. How to dig without damaging the artifacts, what artifacts could be washed and what could not, and what items might be most valuable. Unfortunately, although Maria didn't have anything to do with the crime itself, Reggie had used his relationship with her to learn everything he could about the work archaeologists do in the field."

Lucas kicked me under the table. She'd been right all along. Maria had been part of it.

"She also confessed that she'd brought him to the dig site where we'd been working to show him the tools and techniques we use. Of course, she had no idea what he intended to do with that knowledge.

"She's terribly embarrassed and ashamed of the role she played, even though it was unintentional. And all that is complicated by the fact that what Reggie did was an act of personal betrayal toward her. So I suggested she take some time off to recover."

I have to admit, hearing about it this way, I felt sorry for Maria. She found out her boyfriend was just using her.

Plus, I figured this wouldn't be good for her professional reputation. It might help her be humble, which wouldn't be completely bad, but I wished getting humble hadn't happened to her in quite such a crummy way.

Bernard had driven back to the camp from Nairobi on Monday. On Tuesday, when we were back out on a game drive, he got a call on his cell phone.

When he hung up, he told us the news. The police had caught Reggie the previous night trying to get on a ship at some big harbor in Tanzania. And that morning, Jamison's sons had been found hiding out in some cave—not the Simba Hill cave. Another one. Someone from another Maasai village who was out tending his animals had seen them and turned them in.

"Normally the Maasai would stick together," Bernard said, "but Jamison treated everyone so badly that no one wanted to protect him anymore."

"Their bad karma caught up with them," Lucas said.

Bernard nodded. "It says in the Bible, 'Be sure your sin will find you out.'"

"Same kind of thing," Lucas said.

I called Mom again on Wednesday. I first caught her up on all the news about the criminals and everything.

When I was done with that, she said, "Anything else to report?"

"Yeah, a pretty big thing, too. You know what I

said about the other entrance to the cave, and how they closed it off? Well, this morning Lucas and I got to go out there with Professor Wanjohi and Uncle Geoff to look inside."

"Wow! I'll bet that was cool." Her voice sounded excited for me.

"Well, there was a cool part and a not-so-cool part. We got a chance to go inside. That was the cool part. It was just one big room. There were entrances to some other passages, but they were all collapsed. Anyway, there were walkways around the sides of the room, and that's where we got to stand. But the not-so-cool part was that all the artifacts that were close to the surface have been dug out, and the meeps even removed something that had been on the wall."

"Oh no! That's awful!"

"I know! It's terrible! I got so mad I went stomping around. And that made the professor tell me that it was obvious from the way I reacted that I was cut out to be an archaeologist."

I could hear the smile in Mom's voice when she said, "That must have made you happy. Maybe enough to make up just a little for the missing artifacts?"

Now I was the one to smile. "Maybe just a little. Anyway, Professor Wanjohi said that exploring this second entrance was going to be his next big project. And because Lucas and I helped him discover it, he promised that he'd mention us in the articles he wrote about the cave for archaeological journals."

"Well *that's* pretty sweet!"

"Yeah, I feel really honored to be part of it." To be honest about it, I was really proud that I'd played an important part in what would probably be a major archaeological dig. But I didn't mention that to Mom. I thought she could probably figure it out for herself.

38

Mal d'Afrique

I got to visit the original Simba Hill dig site once more before we left. That time Lucas didn't come with me. She stayed back and spent the afternoon at the pool.

I would never forget the cave, with its beautiful art still on the walls in the passages, the place where I had learned so much about the work I wanted to do when I became an adult. I was glad that I had a chance to look again at the pieces of rock art and artifacts before they got packed up and flown by special plane into Nairobi to be studied and displayed.

On the day we left to start the long trip home, we said good-bye to Professor Wanjohi and Charlie at breakfast. It was really hard.

Charlie put his arms around both Lucas and me at the same time and gave us a big hug. "My parents live in the Twin Cities, and I'll stop to see you when I visit. So don't think you've seen the last of me yet. I'll keep turning up in your lives like a recurring nightmare."

"And I'll meet you when you're doing your archaeological studies," the professor said to me when he was giving me his hug.

I hoped what he said was true. He was one of the greatest men I'd ever met or probably ever would meet in my whole life.

I got tears in my eyes as they left the breakfast table to take off for the dig, and although Lucas isn't as emotional as I am, she seemed pretty sad, too.

Saying good-bye to Sam and Anya was at least as hard as leaving the professor. Probably harder. As we were finishing our packing, they came to our tent and asked if they could come in.

"We have gifts for you," Anya said when they were inside.

Sam handed each of us a small package wrapped in red cloth like the Maasai would wear, tied with another strip of cloth, this one narrow and zebra striped.

"Can we open them now?" Lucas asked.

They both smiled and nodded their heads. "Yes, open them now," Sam said.

Like the packages they came in, the gifts were identical. Wide bracelets showing beaded images of the American flag next to the flag of Kenya, with its green, black, and red stripes and two spears and a shield in the middle.

"They're awesome!" I said. And they were.

"They may be a little big," Sam said. "They were really made for men. But we thought you could keep them somewhere—"

"To remember us by," Anya said. I wondered if all their lives they would be finishing each other's sentences. It was a happy thought.

"We'll *always* remember you!" Lucas said.

Anya said, "Sam and I have decided that you are our favorite lodge guests ever. We hope you can come to our wedding."

She and Sam beamed at us and looked hopeful. Lucas and I both said we'd like to do that. But I knew how much it cost, and I was sure Mom couldn't afford to send me on that trip. And somehow I didn't think that either the Fair Camellia or Allen the Meep would think a wedding was important enough for the kind of money it would take to send us back to Kenya.

We exchanged e-mail and snail mail addresses and phone numbers. Then the two of them helped us take our suitcases to the van, where Bernard and Uncle Geoff stood waiting.

Bernard got our luggage stowed and smiled at the four of us kids as the hugs went on and on.

Finally it was time. Lucas and I got in first, with Uncle Geoff bringing up the rear. Bernard turned the key in the ignition, and we waved at Sam and Anya until the van left the parking lot.

Bernard was looking in the rearview mirror as I wiped my tears away. "So it is difficult for you to leave Kenya?"

"It's terrible. I don't want to go," I said, sobbing just a little.

"We both want to come back," Lucas added.

Uncle Geoff said, "That makes three of us."

I looked out the window through my tears at a herd of impala with their gorgeous handlebar antlers. Beyond them were fields full of wildebeest and zebra. Perched on a rock, not too far away, was a cheetah, waiting to see what would happen.

"Do any of you know the French expression *mal d'Afrique*?" Bernard asked.

"Africa sickness?" Lucas said. Her French is very good.

"Yes," he answered.

She shook her head. "I've never heard of it."

"It does not mean sick *of* Africa," Bernard said. "It means sick *for* Africa. It means missing Africa and longing to come back so much that it's almost like an illness. I believe this feeling is very common."

So there was an actual name for what I was feeling. *Mal d'Afrique.* In the two weeks we'd been there, I felt like I'd come to belong in this place somehow. I'd gotten to know the animals—beginning with that cobra, the great herds of wildebeest, the black rhinos we'd seen that first day, the leopard in the tree. The balloon ride and the gorgeous, moving sea of zebras. That beautiful row of giraffes against the moon. The hippos that splashed in the pool, looking so ridiculous, and the ones that almost trampled us. The lioness who probably saved Lucas's life. And many more that we'd seen in the past two weeks.

I thought of the wonderful people we'd gotten to know and that we would miss. Anya and Sam and Bernard—oh, man, I couldn't even imagine how hard it was going to be to say good-bye to Bernard. And Professor Wanjohi. Even Jeremiah who'd driven us to the balloon ride. I thought of the people in Jamison's village—the women and children with the sad expressions, the boy who had worn the lion head—who could have their village back, and the other Maasai who now maybe would be paid more fairly for their work.

The landscape, too. The acacia trees. The candelabra tree fence. The purple hills. The beautiful, endless sky. The Great Rift Valley.

I knew I had to come back to this place some day. And maybe to other places in Africa. I wanted to go to Tanzania and see Mount Kilimanjaro. To visit South Africa and Botswana. There was so much to see, so much to learn.

But I also knew it might be a while before I could make it back.

In that case, I would just have to be sick for Africa for a good, long time.

Acknowledgments

Writing a book like this, set so far from home and concerning an art form about which I knew little, was a challenge. And this particular manuscript went through untold revisions and permutations, with dozens of readers. Thus I have, as always, many people to thank.

I must begin with my daughter, Annalisa. In addition to smart edits throughout, she provided the first chapter pretty much verbatim. (Read it and you'll see why I like her so well.) A huge contribution. Thank you, thank you, thank you!

Second only to that, much gratitude to the many people who helped me with the subject matter. For information about Kenya and its customs, laws, and people, I turned again and again to Raza Visram, planning operations director for AfricanMecca, a highly acclaimed and multiple-award-winning safari, tour, and beach vacation planning service. Check out their awesome website, www.africanmeccasafaris.com. Raza not only answered every one of literally scores of questions, but he did it always with great courtesy and generosity of spirit. Raza, I am deeply in your debt.

Professor Gilbert Tostevin of the University of Minnesota Department of Anthropology gave unsparingly of his time on several occasions, and provided me with notebooks full of fascinating information about archaeology and an array of articles that informed the text. More than that, he managed to impart to me a warm enthusiasm for a field of which I had been woefully ignorant. I was also fortunate to have input from Minnesota State Archaeologist Scott Anfinson. Though I contacted him late in the process, the information he provided is also reflected in the text.

My brother Steve Runholt filled in a lot of gaps for me about the Great Rift Valley, the Maasai people, and other subjects, based on his two years in Nairobi. Both he and my brother Rusty gave me ideas for some of the best moments in the book. Patty Fares, one of my two marvelous sisters-in-law, a frequent traveler to Kenya and the leader of my own safari trip, helped fill gaps in my memory on a variety of subjects.

All the family members already named, along with my other favorite sister-in-law, Robyn Castellani, read the book while it was in process, in some cases multiple times, and gave me wonderful input. And I relied heavily, as always, on the members of my writers' group, Crème de la Crime: Anne Webb, Carl Brookins, Charlie Rethwisch, Jean Paul, Joan Loshek, Julie Fasciana, Kent Krueger, Mary Monica Pulver, Michael Kac, and Tim Springfield. Special thanks to Charlie, who read through and gave me input on the entire manuscript, and Jean Paul who did the same on a smaller section.

This time there were literally dozens of readers, both young and adult, who read the whole book or parts of it along the way, including Stacy Pinck and other members of an awesome mother/daughter book club based in Minnetonka. Thanks to every single reader! I do want to give special acknowledgment to Jackson Ulstrom and his mother, Andrea, who helped me make several important content decisions.

Finally, thanks to Tina Wexler, my agent, for her input; and to Tracy Gates, heavenly editor, who stayed with me through the long haul.

Susan Runholt went on safari in Kenya just as Kari and Lucas do in *Adventure at Simba Hill*. She didn't see any smugglers, but she did see plenty of giraffes, hippos, and, of course, the lions that give Simba Hill its name. Like her heroines, she ended up with a case of *mal d'Afrique*, which means she hopes to return to Africa soon. Before that, however, she will probably travel somewhere to research her next book, be it near or far from her home in Saint Paul, Minnesota. For more information about Susan Runholt and her books, visit her at www. susanrunholt.com.